Celestial: The Fallen

K.R. Kross

Dedicated to my beautiful wife
who made my white mocha with decaf that one time
because I saw Iron Man 3 instead of realizing
we were already dating in her head.

It was the summer of 2004 and I was in my second year of college for Media Arts & Animation.   I'd wanted to be a comic book artist originally, until I realized I didn't have the patience for drawing a panel at a time while the story lingered in my mind (because outlines are for losers right?), so I shifted my focus to the written word instead.

I'd taken storyboarding classes, drawing classes, photoshop classes and more importantly character design classes when I went home to visit my parents for summer break. We were coming home from a trip to the mall when the song American Pie came on the classic rock station.

I've heard this song plenty of times, it's practically ubiquitous in the cultural memory of American rock music but there was a line that stuck out to me that I'd never really paid attention to until then.

No angel born in Hell
  Could break that Satan's spell
  And as the flames climbed high into the night
  To light the sacrificial rite
  I saw Satan laughing with delight
  The day the music died

"Holeee… SHIT," I thought to myself. The inklings of an idea came to me, the seeds of creative fruit that had the potential to grow into something more. I had a story!

No angel born in Hell.

That single line would consume my entire three-week break as I whipped out my MacBook, sat down at my desk at home and wrote what would become the first draft of my first ever book. From start to finish, I poured words onto the screen and kept pushing out chapter after chapter until I reached my last line and sat back with the realization that I had just written, and completed, an entire coherent fantasy story about a fallen angel in Hell learning to face her greatest challenge... accepting herself as she is and letting go of what she was.

It had intrigue, imaginative scenery inspired by Dante's Divine Comedy, worldbuilding, and interactions with both known and unknown characters from the Christian Bible. Now, I'm not religious, but I believe in things beyond the simple mortal plane, so setting my imagination loose, I drew inspiration wherever I could find it to make an engaging story with entertaining characters that was sure to make me a Million Bucks overnight upon publication! IT WAS FOOLPROOF!!!

I spent the next six months editing and refining my story between classes and whenever else I had time off. I even did my own cover art and EVERYTHING! Once I'd widdled the text down to something I was satisfied with I printed the entire manuscript out at a local Kinkos (do those still exist?) and brought it to an in-school proofer for editing.

Now, let's be real here, with hindsight and years of experience now under my belt, I can safely say that I had absolutely no business publishing this thing at the time. Most seasoned authors would tell you to put that kind of manuscript down and let it stew for a while before going back to it or to simply move on with another project.

At this time in my life, I was in a completely different headspace than I am now. I actually had ambition... and hope... and an optimistic outlook on life in general and actually believed in the good 'ol American Dream! Okay, this is getting depressing, but the point I'm trying to make is that I was driven by optimism and youthful ignorance so I set out to put my work into print someway, somehow.

Now any professional editor, author, or celebrity with common sense will tell you that there are a LOT of publishing scams out there. Self-publishing in 2004-05 was still going through a bit of a credibility crisis due to the fact that such companies usually bilked unsuspecting clients for thousands of dollars upfront in order to publish whatever crap you happen to send their way.

Fortunately, I found a completely different and semi legitimate kind of scam that didn't require my hard earned student loan money upfront. I clicked the link online and saw that they catered to 'NEW AUTHORS' and didn't charge anything for publishing, so I submitted my manuscript for an evaluation because why not? Not a week later I got a response that said they would 'love to publish' my work, so they sent over a contract and I was thrilled, but also terrified.

Ever vigilant, I read every line very carefully making sure I wasn't surrendering my rights, other than publishing and kept my eye out for any hidden fees, but to my relief, everything was on the up and up. I signed the contract and I was on my way to the NY Times Bestseller list boiiii!

After going back and forth with the formatted text and cover proofs, I finalized the print file and gave my okay for publishing and within a month I had my first copies of my book in hand and I couldn't be happier. Of course, I soon learned what the actual catch was of this particular scam... you (the author) had to pay for literally EVERYTHING ELSE because the publisher wasn't going to.

Marketing? Out of pocket. Extra copies of your book to sell yourself? Out of pocket at wholesale price, which wasn't that great considering the retail price of most mass market books was the same if not less than the wholesale price of MY book. Book signings? Yep, you guessed it, out of pocket. All the things I needed to get any kind of exposure for my work cost money that I just didn't have. And of course this was before the days of Facebook and Amazon Ads.

I still sold a few copies to friends and family of course and even got it converted to eBook (for a fee), but ultimately my masterpiece didn't sell nearly as well as I thought it would. I was crushed, defeated, wandering aimlessly through the desolate wastes of Wage Slavery, desperate for release when I knew I should be drinking Mai-Tai's with J.K. Rowling and making fun of poor people on a gentrified beach somewhere. But still, some eternal spark of hope lingered in my blackened heart, so I kept writing.

I have other manuscripts, of course, other stories scratching at the inside of my brain waiting to be unleashed upon an unsuspecting public, and have since discovered the joys of Fan Fiction (::cough:: AKyloDarkly83 on Ao3 ::cough::) but as of this writing, it's 2019 and Self Publishing is a completely different beast. With certain large online booksellers dominating all creative markets up to and including your home electronics, I can put whatever honied words I wish into the ether of Cyberspace and there's nothing anyone can do to stop me!

So why then, am I re-printing this novella, my first ever book? One, because I'm still desperate for money and this is as shameless a cash grab as I can make it and maybe this will pick up a few bucks, or 'quid' depending on what side of the pond you're on, while I dance and curse my way into Bestseller status. Two, because it's great practice for setting up the process of printing my own books, I'm a huge DIYer and honestly a bit of a control freak. Three, Maybe I just want my fellow writers out there to know that it's okay to dream big and fail because no matter what... you learn something from it.

I'm releasing this magnificent manuscript back out into the wild as a time capsule of my early publishing life, a window into my thought process, and as a warning. That's right, a warning to my fellow writers. This book is AWFUL, I mean, it's BAD.

Like, film student movie but in written form BAD.

Yeah, yeah I've heard all that 'we are our own worst critics' stuff time and time again, but honestly, going back through this I was cringing so hard I had to break my rule of not rewriting some parts of it, and in fact have decided that I'm actually going to rewrite this entire story into something worthy of my readers sensibilities. What I'm saying is the proper mindset for going into this should be to read it as a parody, a tragic comedy of errors, a bad B-Movie in book form. This book is a master class in HOW NOT TO WRITE. I promise you, you'll learn and, hopefully, enjoy it so much more if you proceed with that mindset than without.

And hey, if you happen to like it how it is, that's cool too. Maybe your kids will enjoy it for entirely different reasons, you never know. Either way, enjoy the journey because that's what writing is and always has been. Just like Celestial's fall into Hell, it may start rough, but once you find your footing, it can take you places that you can only dream of and reveal something about yourself that you never knew before, and maybe, just maybe it'll inspire you to write that next bestseller that gets turned into a shitty movie franchise no one asked for.

In that spirit, friends, I invite you to read on at your own risk and benefit.

-K. R. Kross

P.S.

Your negative Amazon reviews can't possibly hurt me any more than I've hurt myself.

Trust me. :)

Introduction

It is written, that in the beginning, God created Heaven and Earth, and of his will, so too came the sun and the moon. God then went on to create all the beasts that roamed the Earth and all the plants that sprang from the ground. At last, God created man, and from man, woman. This act of creation was overseen not only by God but also by those closest to him, his own children... the angels.

It is these angels who command responsibility for guarding the kingdom of Heaven and to guide the souls of mankind so that they do not become lost to temptation on their journey through life. From the beginning, these divine beings have watched as humanity multiplied and gave rise to a mighty empire only to turn their gifts of intelligence and passion on each other. They were soon consumed by war and hatred and some began to turn their backs on their creator.

Angels are not altogether different from humankind for they too feel emotions. Joy, love, and reverence are but the finest emotions but others like sadness, anger, and pride began to manifest. For a time they could control these feelings, but every once upon a dying star they are blinded so greatly by their emotions, they can commit the most human of sins.

When a mortal sins, their souls become weighed down by their actions. If their sin is great enough their soul risks falling into Hell. A mortals sin comes not without the chance of redemption upon which they can return to the Shining City. Angels, however, have such an intimate bond with God himself, when they commit a mortal sin; their very divinity is put in danger. When an angel commits such an act as to bring down the anger of their lord and master, they are struck down like flies and fall from the white city into the darkest pit of damnation.

Lucifer was one such creature.

It was his overwhelming jealousy of man and his substantial pride that drove him from the Garden of Eden and sent him to the darkness, from whence his unholy kingdom arose. Once a protector of humankind, Lucifer has since relinquished his divine title in shame, and as the supreme ruler of the suffering lands, all who fall into his world can never escape his grasp.

Others have joined the Dark Prince over time, especially those who worshipped him instead of God, but there will soon be another angel who will realize for herself the horrible fate that awaits her as she falls from her divine home into the black pit.

Her name is Celestial, and this is her story.

CHAPTER ONE

Exile

Her once divine flesh is all but burned away as Celestial plummets through the thick smoke that is the entrance to the Dark Lands. She tumbles through the air like a fowl that has been shot from the sky, while the feathers on her wings tear from her bones. She screams and pleads for mercy to her God in heaven, from whom she is now parted, but is met only with the sound of the acrid air rushing by her ears. The angel falls closer to the unholy soil of Hell's table; now engulfed in agony, she slams into the ground like a falling star, another broken soul amidst the vast plain of craters. Given that she is spirit she cannot die from such an impact, but the pain that courses through her body is all too real.

Celestial, caked in dirt and charred flesh writhes in agony as she attempts to sit up. Only pained shrieks escape her dry, broken lips.

"Why, God? What have I done to anger you so?" she cries. The very breeze that rushes past is like a thousand blades cutting her skin as she struggles to look around. Crawling over the rim of the crater left in her wake she sees only rivers of lava and plumes of fire scorching the already barren clay. Black mountains rise through the blood-red sky, spanning as far as her once blue eyes can see. A smoke so dark it seemed to absorb all light, billows from their cores through natural vents but there are also the sounds.

Soul wrenching screams of agony and sorrow wash across the plains like an ocean of suffering as mass fields of condemned slaves eternally labor for their demonic masters. She watched in bleary-eyed silence as the masters cruelly punished their slaves with lead-weighted whips. The foulest curses and blackest of oaths issued from their bloodstained mouths as they drove the pathetic masses beyond their limitations, not caring for their suffering.

She took only a few steps before a massive winged beast roared overhead before swooping down to grab a claw full of unfortunate victims before whisking them away to some unspeakable fate. She turned to flee from the terrifying sights only to see other, smaller beasts chewing and fighting over their still living victims. Terror was her master now and she knew there was nowhere to run but she ran anyway.

Empty burrows dot the land between the fields of laborers and soon she finds one that is remote enough to allow her to breathe. She starts to inspect the damage done to her body and weeps with ever-growing sorrow. Her right wing is broken almost in half and the feathers that once gave her flight are all but fallen from their stems. Naked and covered in grime, char and brimstone ash, Celestial is further shocked to see what other changes had been forced upon her.

An angel is pure and whole in every respect, they are children of God and have not the need for the faculties of humans but as she looks at her chest and between her thighs she sees only the original sin of a mortal woman. No longer is she a creature of God and no longer does his light burn in her eyes. As a fresh wave of agony washes over her, Celestial pulls her knees to her chest and cries in the darkest corner of the burrow. She wanted nothing more than to disappear into the shadows, to melt away like her once radiant flesh and be lost to the Void.

She prayed in her Angelic tongue, though each word came out as a new blasphemy that only brought further pain. For the moment she found safety in the small burrow and perhaps, she thought, she could hide from the worst fates in the Dark Lands, but it is a foolish heart to think that one's descent into Hell might go unnoticed.

***

With the skittering of claws, Celestial awakens from her sleep. She scans the burrow with renewed fear, unsure of what she had heard. Was it a dream? Was it a trick of the mind in this evil place? She didn't want to know the answer, instead, she huddled against the back wall and waited. Nothing happened.

"W-who's there? Bring yourself into the light so that my eyes may see who stalks me!" Her demand is met with silence; she continues walking. From the darkness, a seductive female voice speaks out to Celestial.

"Well my sister, let it be known that we have laid eyes upon a "fallen one," and a fresh one by the looks of it." Another female voice from across the canyon replies, "Fresh indeed, sister! She is ripe to play with, it would seem," the voices deviously chuckle in the dark.

Nervously, Celestial calls out to the sisters in the shadows, "Who are you? Why do you speak these things about me?"

"It is rare to find a fallen angel, like yourself, around here. My sister and I have been blessed if one can call it that." From the shadows above, two winged figures drop to the ground, landing with a great thud. Due to their sin, souls in Hell weigh nearly ten times what they would weigh as mortals on Earth. The two figures slowly walk into the light with a seductive stride. They are both similar in appearance with long flowing black hair and deeply tanned skin. They have leathery bat-like wings that stand nearly twice their height and torn cloth draped over their voluptuous bodies. A series of brandings wind their way down each sister's arm and are composed of demonic symbols that seem to read like a story of their lives. Bony ridges flow across their foreheads, and small horns protrude from them at a subtle angle. For creatures of Hell, these two female demons are deceptively beautiful in appearance; one would say they are the temptresses of the underworld.

Celestial takes small, timid steps backward as the sisters approach her. The demoness on the left steps forward and says, "By what sin do you find yourself in this forsaken land, angel? Was it excessive pride, jealousy, anger?"

Slowly creeping backward, Celestial answers, "It is no business of yours, demon." Visibly annoyed, the demoness sneers at Celestial and says to her, "I think it is my business, angel trash! This is my world and you will do as I say! Are those not our rules, Jezebel?"

Jezebel, the second girl, steps forward with a hostile sneer and replies, "Yes Crissella. Those are our rules!"

"I obey only God himself and none other. Stay away from me, sinful creatures!" shouts Celestial as she prepares to run away.

"Look where you are and honestly tell me God would help you here! Jezebel, grab her!"

"With much pleasure, my sister," Jezebel replies as she lunges toward the frightened angel. Celestial tries to jump out of the way but the demoness hastily grabs hold of her. The angel struggles to free herself from her captor but her weakened state prevents her from overpowering Jezebel.

"Certainly, you wish you could fly now don't you, angel bitch?" taunts Jezebel. Meanwhile, Crissella briskly strides forward and grabs Celestial's face with her demonic claws. She leans forward until she is inches from the angel's face and says to her, "You have much to learn about living in the forsaken land. The first lesson is…" Crissella cuts Celestial's cheek with her claw, "…your pain is my pleasure!" A drop of clear fluid glowing with an aura of light drips from Celestial's wound, when Crissella continues to say, "The second lesson is, fresh angel blood is considered the finest of delicacies among the demon masters here." She then licks the open wound on Celestial's face with her forked lizard-like tongue. Tensing from a rush of sudden pleasure, Crissella continues.

"Mmm, extraordinary! I haven't felt such a rush of ecstasy since the last dying star!"

"What of our time spent in bed together, sister; when my flesh pleased your flesh?" utters Jezebel.

"Oh please, you flatter yourself. This is ten times more invigorating than the simple pleasures of the flesh." Once again Crissella moves in closer to Celestial's face until she is a mere breathe away from her. Holding her hand behind Celestial's neck Crissella says:

"As an angel, I understand that you have never experienced pleasures of the flesh. Here's a taste of what you've been missing." Crissella slowly and tenderly presses her lip against Celestial's; she winces in disgust. Finally Celestial ends the kiss by biting Crissella's lip. The demon woman lurches back as Celestial shouts:

"Get away from me, demonic whore!" Celestial then kicks Crissella further away and manages to throw Jezebel to the ground. She quickly flees from the sisters as Crissella stands up again.

"Bitch! I will enjoy tearing her wings from her body!" The enraged demoness lets out a blood-curdling screech as she launches herself into the air with a powerful flap of her black wings. Jezebel regains her composure and proceeds to follow her sister and their prey.

With feathers trailing from her damaged wings, Celestial runs from the demonesses who chase her, but the sisters, with all their unholy strength, easily keep pace from the air.

"Fleeing will not save you from suffering, fallen one! You cannot escape the fury of Hell!" Crissella shouts as she swoops down to tackle her victim. Dropping from the sky like a bomb, the demoness slams into Celestial from behind, dragging her to the ground as they both roll to a stop in a cloud of dust. Celestial struggles with all her might to crawl away from Crissella but she clamps her powerful thighs around the angel's frail waist. With one powerful motion, Crissella backhands the rebellious angel across her face, sending clear blood flying from the wound in her cheek. Upon impact with the foul soil, the clear angel blood boils and sears, changing to a pitch black color, like that which flows through the veins of all the demons in Hell.

Jezebel promptly lands next to her sister with the fallen angel in her possession. She stands over the two and says to Crissella:

"I think we need to finish the cycle and turn her into the thing she fears most! Do you not agree, sister?"

"Yes, Jezebel, I do agree. What better way to punish an angel than to make her an enemy of God!" Crissella grins as she holds down her opponent.

"What are you going to do to me? Please don't hurt me, I beg of you!" pleads Celestial.

"It's too late for you, child. It's time that you understand what it truly means to be forsaken!"

The sisters both take hold of Celestial and flip her over like a fish. Grabbing hold of her dying wings, with one mighty pull they viciously tear them from Celestial's back.

The scourged angel screams in agony as she falls onto her side. Celestial's clear blood gushes from her back and onto the cursed soil, which causes it to instantly boil and transform into black ooze. The puddle of blood surrounds the twitching angel, almost as if it were alive itself, and slowly the black fluid begins taking the shape of a pair of wings behind her, much like those of the two sisters. The wings quickly harden into a leathery pile while the remaining blood rapidly slurps back into Celestial's body, giving her pale flesh a deep brown tan. Her once radiant blonde hair drains of all color to become black as night, and her fingernails and toes stretch and crack as they deform into thin claws. Bony ridges crack and stretch from her head, and two small horns break through her scalp.

Moments pass when Celestial finally opens her eyes; their pale white color has drastically shifted to a deep crimson red that glows as if a fire burned within. After regaining consciousness, she quickly rolls and brings herself to her feet. She flexes and stretches her muscles as newfound strength courses through her naked body. All her scratches and bruises from the abuse she's taken from the fall and the sisters' attack have rapidly disappeared. Crissella slowly walks toward her and puts a hand upon her shoulder saying:

"Welcome to our family… my sister." Jezebel giggles deviously as Celestial looks around at the scorched terrain with a dumbfounded stare; then, with a mild smirk on her face, she responds, "It's good to be home… sister."

CHAPTER TWO

Journey to the Master

The stifling air blasts the trio of demonic sisters as they stride across the broken land. They march, mile after mile, toward the unholy palace of Satan himself. Wiping the sweat from her brow, Jezebel complains to her sister Crissella:

"Explain again, sister why we travel by foot and not by flight? It would be much faster, and would sooner relieve us from this damned heat!"

"We don't fly because our sibling has not the strength in her wings to fly. She must rest for a time before she can make use of them." Crissella says while striding with an unyielding pace. From behind, Celestial comments to her sisters:

"It would seem I've found a somewhat beneficial use for these wings after all, don't you?" Crissella looks back and smirks at Celestial, who has her wings wrapped around her naked body like a cloak to shield her from the harsh environment.

Continuing their march towards the distant palace, Celestial's curiosity about the prince of darkness gets the better of her.

"So is your master, Satan, truly as horrible as everyone says he is?" To her side, Jezebel replies, "He is a self-indulged tyrant, with no better use for his time than to have is way with the likes of us!

"Silence your tongue, Jezebel, he's no worse than any other demon you've shared a bed with!" snaps Crissella.

"Perhaps, but that fact makes him no less of a bastard!" Jezebel says in return to the comment. Celestial seems somewhat surprised by how the two sisters converse about their master, so she says to them:

"I can't believe you two would speak about the Prince of Darkness in such a manner as this! Are you not afraid of him?" Crissella and Jezebel look at each other with an uneasy glance, then Crissella turns to Celestial and replies:

"Only when we are standing in his presence are we truly frightened of him."

"Why only in his presence, do you fear him?" asks Celestial. Crissella stops and looks at her with quivering eyes, and says in a trembling tone:

"Rarely do we see his true form… and when we do, we wish that we had not." The trio stands in silence for a moment, as if pondering what lies ahead of them; they march on once again.

The black palace on the horizon becomes closer to them with each further step. The towering spires pierce the sky with their cast iron turrets and their flaming windows, where souls of the damned patrol the burning hallways, forever ablaze and eternally suffering. There are statues of horrible creatures standing in front of the palace that is constructed from the tortured bodies of slaves who failed to keep pace in their assigned fields of labor. The statues are called the "moaning tributes", named so because of the endless moans of agony and suffering that emanate from the captive slaves.

The demonesses walk up to the massive Iron Gate that is encrusted with skulls and bones from many kinds of creatures, and before they knock to enter into the black castle, Jezebel says to Crissella:

"Shouldn't we warn her about Eva? She may not know of her, not many souls do."

Crissella glances at Jezebel and then at Celestial and says, "Perhaps, we should."

"Who is Eva?" asks Celestial. Crissella explains the story to Celestial.

"Not long ago, our master tried to construct his own version of "The Garden," in which he attempted to recover the slightest piece of his lost divinity. However, nothing grew from the burnt and broken ground, and all of his furnishings and statues would fade to dust within moments after their contact with the arid soil. He was devastated by failure and felt an excruciating desire to end his life, knowing that there was no hope in such an act. He then decided to take things one step further. He reasoned that if he couldn't have a garden of his own, then he would at least spend eternity with a creature of exceptional status. Much like Adam, Lucifer took a rib from his own body and cast it into the garden, thus creating a partner of his own who would be called his Queen."

"Oh my…" utters Celestial as she stares in shock from hearing the story, "… so what happened after that?"

"Well, in a twist of universal irony, Eva was born from the only divine bone left in Satan's body, and so she is beautiful like an angel, but her heart is as black and cold as his own." Explains Jezebel.

"Never have I been aware of a Queen of Hell, and never have I felt such sympathy for the poor creature, Satan." Celestial says.

"Do not sympathize for his black heart! You will learn to hate his existence just as my sister and I have hated him," growls Crissella with a small tear rolling down her cheek. "Let us enter. He will surely desire to meet you." Crissella grabs the carved bone knocker on the door and slams it against the hollow surface several times. A moment passes when the door shakes with a loud clunk then slowly creeps open. A blast of freezing cold air chills Celestial to the bone as the girls walk through the large doorway. A small imp-like creature jumps from behind the door and greets the trio.

"Ah, Crissella, Jezebel welcome back! It looks like my two favorite temptresses brought a new friend with them, a fresh one too!" The imp scurries behind Celestial and reaches his frail clawed hands between her wings to squeeze her buttocks. She quickly whips around and shouts at the hunch-backed creature.

"Take your filthy claws off of me, you little rat!" Crissella stomps over to the imp, shouting:

"Sorthen, did I not warn you about approaching my sisters in such a way?"

The grotesque little imp sharply looks around, and replies, "You said that you would severely hurt me, mistress. That is what I am hoping for after all!"

With a look of revulsion upon her face, Crissella walks away saying, "You're a disgusting little troll! Leave us be." As the trio of demonesses walks away, Sorthen shouts to them:

"It's only a matter of time mistress! You'll have to break to your will eventually!"

As the girls walk through the dark hallway, Crissella says to Celestial, "You must excuse that walking heap of maggot waste. He is persistent in trying to make us hurt him, so that he may feel sexual gratification. Feel free to keep him away by any means necessary."

The light in the hallway glows increasingly brighter as the girls walk closer and closer to the main entrance hall. The dank and corroding columns of brimstone slowly switch to pillars of burnt marble and golden statues as they enter the sinfully glorious main hall. With a ceiling that raises nearly ten stories to a central point, the hall is very similar to many gothic style churches on Earth. The shape of the floor is circular and each of the walls flows with waterfalls of blood that run through a series of channels to unite into a red moat that surrounds Satan's black throne, and the throne of his queen, Eva. Aqueducts that cut across the ceiling direct molten lava from the mountains outside through the interior of the palace, flowing to an unknown destination.

Celestial clenches her wings tighter around her body as she shivers from the chill, "How is it possible that with all this lava, the wind feels so cold?"

"They say that the palace is cursed with the same warmth as the heart of he who created it. Within our master's chest there beats a cold heart, and within his palace there blows an equally cold breeze." Informs Crissella.

Jezebel says to Celestial, "We must call for him now. When he arrives, I must warn you that he may take any form at will. Whatever form he chooses you must avoid his eyes, no matter how seemingly innocent his appearance may be."

"Why must I not look into his eyes?" asks a confused Celestial.

"Trust my words, I know what I speak of," replies Jezebel as she gets down on one knee in preparation for his arrival. Celestial follows their example and crouches down on one knee. They all put their heads down and Crissella makes the call.

"Master, we have brought someone for you to meet! We request your presence before us." A moment of uneasy silence passes by when suddenly a thundering voice with the boom of an army speaks out. The voice has such a deep tone, the very foundation of the palace shakes with every word.

"Who have you brought before me?"

"We have brought before you, a Fallen One from the silver kingdom above. We have since turned her into one of your faithful minions master!"

"I must have a closer look at this 'fallen one' before I deem her faithful to me!"

With their heads still down, the sisters, remain motionless as thunderous crackling echoes throughout the palace. With an unholy roar, a massive ball of fire bursts before the throne, followed by a loud thud that shakes the floor. The girls continue to hold their heads down, yet they are aware that Satan himself is standing before them. The halo of fire that surrounds his body pierces the air with its sickening orange glow. The beast begins walking toward the sisters, with each step shaking the ground. Each breath he takes pulsates throughout their bones until he comes to a stop, directly before them.

Celestial is breathing very heavily, as she feels the heat radiating from his body. Fear is streaked across her face as she holds her head low, but she is suddenly greeted with a pair of perfectly shined leather dress shoes standing before her. The glow from the fire has disappeared, and the demon's terrible voice has changed to that of a mortal man.

"Stand up, darling, let me have a look at you." says the man with a modest tone.

Celestial looks over at Crissella who mouths to her, "Do not look into his eyes!"

Celestial slowly stands up as the man takes a few steps back. Avoiding direct eye contact, Celestial glances at the man's general form and is surprised to see a seemingly handsome man wearing a clean cut, striped suit. He has short, black hair and wears a boyish grin on his face as he lets out a fox whistle toward the girl.

"You sure are a pretty one aren't you? You're much more beautiful than I give most angels credit for. I'm surprised, I thought you were all big, butch warriors of God, ready to tear demons apart, limb from limb. Heh-heh, who'd have thought you would actually be hot? What's your name, young lady?"

"Celestial is my name." She answers with a mild tone. The man walks around Celestial, admiring her sensuous curves then he says to her, "Why don't you open up those wings for me, Celestial? You needn't be shy, the female form is a natural wonder to behold."

Timidly, Celestial unfolds her wings, exposing her nakedness to the man who is called The Prince of Darkness.

"Mm, mm, mm… very nice. You've certainly got what it takes to be one of my minions… however, I'm still not sure if you're truly faithful to my cause or not."

"I am faithful to you and only you, master. My God has abandoned me from his presence. I no longer have any will to obey him." Celestial states as a tear of sorrow roll down her cheek.

"I want you to look me in the eyes and tell me you're faithful to me, and only to me."

Celestial hesitates for a moment before deciding to do what as wishes, or else she might face the horrible consequences. Celestial slowly brings her head up to look into his eyes. Her eyes lock onto his, and for a moment her fear has ceased.

Without warning, Celestial screams in agony as she falls to her knees, clenching the sides of her head. The other sisters hold their ears, but they have already begun crying from the pain inflicted by the sheer pitch of the shriek. She grabs at her head as if trying to protect it from an invisible creature, burrowing into her skull. Celestial drops her forehead to the ground, directly in front of Satan's feet, prostrating her, when he utters, "Welcome to the family."

CHAPTER THREE

Playtime

In the midst of a dimly lit room, Celestial lies unconscious upon a large bed; she tosses and turns in the fit of a horrible nightmare. The rolling and thrashing come to a peak when she springs up from the bed, yelling:

"Stay away from me!" Heavily breathing and drenched with sweat, she quickly realizes that she is awake and glances around the unfamiliar bedchamber.

From a dark corner, Jezebel's nasal voice speaks out to her, "Well it's about time you awoke! Babysitting a sleeping angel bores me to tears."

"Where am I? What happened to me?" asks Celestial as she holds her head.

"This is where my sister and I sleep. We're in the east wing of the palace on the 13th floor. I warned you about his black heart; he forced you to look into his eyes, knowing very well what you would see. His true form is barely enough for his own minions to handle. That shape would instantly destroy a man if they were to lay their mortal eyes upon it."

"How long have I been asleep?" asks the weary Celestial.

"Who knows? Time has no meaning down here so I wouldn't worry your pretty little head over it." Jezebel replies as she strokes Celestials damp hair.

At that moment, Crissella walks through the tall wooden door and sees that Celestial has awoken, "Ah, it would appear that you've collected yourself. Did you sleep well?" she asks with a sarcastic manner.

"Hardly. There were horrible images flashing before my mind's eye… images of him. He had the face of a snake's skull and twisted horns curling behind his back. His body was burnt and scarred from countless weapons."

Crissella says to her weary sister, "Well, you had better get used to not sleeping well, that is the way of all nightmares in this place. There is a sheer lack of positive energy here; so pleasant dreams can never be transmitted from the outer universe, especially once you've seen his true form. You'll learn to cope, over time."

Crissella hurries over to her dresser and shuffles through her various accessories and clothes. Celestial stands up from her bed and explores the room, glancing at the statues and pendants lining the wall; she finally asks the sisters:

"When I saw him… I noticed there were three living faces, stapled to his body. Who are they?"

The sister's glance at each other with a confused look, then Jezebel says to Celestial, "You do not know? Hasn't your God informed you of the fate that befell the greatest sinners on Earth?"

"Well… we do not speak directly to God… he speaks to us through a Seraph that guards his chamber, they are the highest order of angels. He has never spoken openly about the ways of Hell and the sinners who burn here."

"Surprising. Never would I have guessed that angels don't actually talk to their God; there seems to be a certain irony here. Anyhow, the two faces upon his shoulders… the one on the left is the face of Brutus, the great Roman betrayer of Julius Caesar. The face on his right is that of Vlad Dracul, known more widely by the mortals as "Vlad the Impaler"… the self-proclaimed Antichrist. The face on his arm is that of Judah of Iscariot, the betrayer of your Christ."

"You mean to say they are forever attached to Satan's body?"

"Yes… our master is, of course, the greatest of all betrayers, so it is only fitting that he wears the souls of those most like himself upon his forsaken flesh," replies Jezebel.

Crissella continues shuffling through her dresser until she finally stumbles upon something.

"Aha, I found it!"

Celestial asks her, "What have you found?"

Crissella replies, "Your shirt for tonight." She pulls out a small black shirt with a stylized cartoon devil kitten on the front with the words "Sinner" emblazoned in day-glow flames beneath it.

Celestial stares at it in disbelief then says to Crissella, "You must... be kidding."

Crissella glances down at it and states, "It seemed cute to me when I stole it."

Celestial lightly chuckles to herself at the thought of a demon temptress of Hell holding such a cute shirt. Once she regains her composure she asks Crissella:

"So... what happens tonight?"

"We are going out!" replies Crissella with an excited smile on her face.

Celestial rolls her eyes around in confusion at the remark.

"Where could we possibly go? Is this not Hell, where we are supposed to burn for all eternity?"

"Perhaps I should rephrase my statement. We are going up... to the mortal world. As temptresses, we are free to come and go as we please, and tonight I crave... companionship."

"My favorite kind of companionship, my sister," says Jezebel. With the flick of her wrist, a quick burst of fire burns around her, and once the smoke clears, she takes on the appearance of a mortal female. Her wings have vanished, and her skin is fair instead of ash dark, and her shredded rags have transformed into a sultry cocktail dress that would be welcomed at any nightclub.

Crissella performs the same motion and takes the appearance of another woman, her eyes slanted and vibrant. Her rags have changed into a pair of black leather pants and a silk top. Celestial is amazed at the transformation and immediately asks:

"How did you do that?"

Crissella replies, "It's quite simple... imagine yourself as a mortal woman wearing whatever you wish, and will it to be so! The power of Hell is very easy to control with your mind."

Celestial looks at the cute black shirt in her hands and tries to envision herself as a mortal woman, of which she has no experience becoming. With a puff of fire, the fallen angel is engulfed in a cloud of prickly heat when the space around her clears. She is wearing the little black "sinner" t-shirt and a short leather miniskirt.

She looks herself over and exclaims, "Amazing! Never could I imagine anything like this down here."

"It would seem you have good control over your thoughts, my sister. Your outfit is deliciously provocative," exclaims Crissella.

"We had better raise the portal, so that we may have a fair selection before they all return home," says Jezebel. The sisters walk toward the center of the room, where Crissella casts a spell in her satanic tongue. Within moments, a floor-length ring of fire materializes out of the air. The image of a New York City nightclub shows in the center of the ring. Crissella asks her sisters:

"How does New York sound, sisters?" She motions for Celestial to step into the ring and says to her, "See for yourself, Celestial."

"Are you sure? Will people see us?"

"Don't worry; we will enter through an alleyway, where it is dark. After you, sister!" Crissella says to Celestial as she holds her hand towards the ring of fire. Celestial cautiously steps forward into the portal, and in an instant, she finds herself in the dark alleyway, exactly where the gateway showed her. Looking around for a moment or two, Celestial glances back to see her two sisters emerging from the portal as the flaming ring dissipates from existence behind them.

Crissella steps forward and says to Celestial, "Now we may have some fun! You seem as though you could use some." The trio of sisters strides out of the alleyway toward the back door of the club, where a large brick house of a bouncer stands watch. As the girls approach him he steps down from the doorstep and says:

"And where do you think you ladies are going tonight? The line is on the other side."

Crissella walks up to the bouncer and puts her hand on his cheek, instantly releasing an extremely powerful dose of pheromones, and then she says to him, "I know… but I wanted to avoid all of those people by coming in through the back, instead!"

The pheromones are so potent that they easily cloud the bouncer's sense of judgment, leading him to say, "Hey, no problems, ladies! Go inside and have yourselves a good ol' time."

"Thank you, kind sir; let's go, girls," Crissella says, as the trio walks into the club. The inside of the club is dark and muggy from all the people who are packed into it. The techno music blares while strobe lights flash in a synchronized pattern; masses of people dance and gyrate on the main floor as the bartenders twirl bottles and pour large quantities of alcohol. As the sisters walk around the outer edge of the club, Celestial stops for a moment to catch her breath.

She says, "What is wrong with me? My heart is racing, and my breathing grows heavy!"

Crissella steps close to her frightened sister and says, "You are feeling lust; one of the great feelings a woman could have! Come, let us find you a mortal to satisfy your desires."

Jezebel notices a group of clubgoers just off the dance floor and says, "Look at those creatures there. Their hearts already ache with desire."

"Then let us make our move," Crissella says as she begins walking toward them.

"What are we to do with them?" asks a concerned Celestial.

"You feel lust do you not? We are here to satisfy that craving! Do you prefer male or female?"

"Excuse me?"

"That's right, you're new to carnal pleasure. Let us keep it simple, I'll get a nice strong man for you. Jezebel prefers the ladies."

Jezebel sticks her tongue out at her sister as she approaches the small group.

One of the men on the far end takes notice of their approach and downs another swig of his beer and then stands up to greet them.

"Hi there, ladies; you look like you could use some company. My friends and I were just about to go home alone, again… but if you would like to join us…"

With a peppy, valley girl tone Crissella says to the man, "Really? Like, oh my God, we were just about to go home too, heh-heh. So like, what are your names and stuff?"

"Riiiight…Oh, uh this blonde fella over here is John, the short stud next to him is Nathan, and I'm Dan. Your names would be?"

"Well like, my friends totally call me Crissy, and my sister here is Jessica, and my other sister behind me is Celeste. We come from a big family."

"That's… nice… so anyway, would you like to go out back for some… fresh air, or something?" Dan says with a nervous twitch.

"Um, actually, I wanted to speak to that lovely young lady behind you," Jezebel added as she pointed.

The woman had short shoulder length hair as she eyed her with a smirk.

Dan laughs, "Ha, that's my sister, Trish." He turns to her then, "Hey sis, I think this one's your type."

"Yes, she certainly is," Trish says with a languorous look.

Crissella runs her finger down Dan's chest, releasing another dose of pheromones as she says, "Well Danny, now that that's cleared up, I could use some…" Crissy looks up and down his body and continues, "… fresh air!" The two lock arms together and quickly make haste for the exit to the back alley.

Jezebel and Celestial remain behind with the other two men and Trish, who are still at the bar. Jessica looks at her chosen prey and smiles. Celestial can feel the sway she holds on the woman who stumbles for words.

"Uh, I think I need to go get some... fresh air... too. Do you, uh want to come with?" she asks Jezebel.

She quickly replies, "I don't know... I might need a drink first."

The man called Nathan, apparently under her sway as well, hastily hands his drink over to the vixen and says, "Here take mine, it's on me."

"Thanks, stud, that'll do!" Jezebel eyes Trish, then Celestial, as she walks with her toward the back door to meet Crissella and her new boy toy; before stepping outside, she looks back and winks at her.

Celestial finds herself alone with the remaining two men, who both are apparently enthralled by the pheromones when the one called John tries to initiate an intelligent conversation between them.

"So, you girls are sisters huh?"

"Oh, yeah we're sisters. We decided to have a girl's night out tonight, so here we are... or were. It seems my sisters are quite easily distracted."

"Yeah, I suppose. It's no surprise though... you're all very beautiful."

"Super beautiful, I mean the most beautiful," Nathan adds, chewing his bottom lip.

Her cheeks flush with warmth as another feeling rushes through her, compassion.

"You honestly think I'm beautiful?" Celestial asks in earnest.

Then John says to her, "Celeste, it should be a sin to be that beautiful!"

Quickly, the rush of pleasure and happiness drains from Celestial's face as the word "sin" echoes in her mind. Her placid smile rapidly fades as she looks away from the two of them and then towards the door in the back.

"Um, I just remembered that I have somewhere to go. I must see to it that my sisters don't get themselves into too much trouble." She briskly walks away from the bar and toward the rear exit to join her sisters.

"Wait, what's wrong? Was it something I said? I didn't mean anything by it, I swear," pleads John as Celestial steps out of the door in the back. In the alleyway, Crissella and Jezebel are both pressed up against the wall as they passionately make-out with their chosen partners. On the verge of full-fledged sexual intercourse, articles of clothing begin to fall off as they squirm and fondle each other against the cold brick wall.

"Hell certainly has a powerful influence on mortal flesh." Celestial says as she walks toward the end of the alleyway.

While smooching Dan, Crissella says to Celestial, "You have no idea, sister," Daniel kisses up and down her neck as she asks, "Where's your partner, Celestial? The plan was perfectly set up."

Holding her arms, Celestial tearfully responds, "Plans change. I would rather be alone right now." She begins crying to herself as Crissella stares in disbelief.

"Damn it. Be gone from me." She says as she pushes Daniel away.

"Whoa, wait a minute, I thought you wanted me all over you?" he says with a confused manner. Crissella puts her hand to his forehead and sends a burst of energy through him that renders him unconscious, causing him to fall to the ground. She then walks over to Celestial and says to her:

"Listen, I understand you feel revulsion toward these feelings in your heart; you must understand that you are no longer an angel, Celestial! You are a temptress in the kingdom of Hell; one who does not refuse their desires. Trust in what I say; to satisfy a desire is to bring peace to your heart. To deny your desire is to bring suffering unto yourself; you lower yourself to the level of the slaves who work in the fields. Is that what you seek, suffering?"

"I was an angel, and lust in my heart brought suffering unto me. To mingle with mortals in this manner would have surely cast me from God's graces. And forever did I fear that day." Crissella grabs Celestial's shoulder and turns her around.

"Look at where you are! You have been cast out, Celestial; regardless of how pure you were, you have been cast out nonetheless. Why do you continue to hold on to a family that turned their backs on you?"

Celestial stands silent as she ponders Crissella's words. She then looks over at Jezebel and sees her playing a suspicious game with Trish's mind.

"Do you love me, baby?" She says.

"More than anything in the world," she replies.

"Would you do anything for me?"

"Anything at all my mistress."

"Would you kill for me?"

Trish's eyes are glazed and wide as she ponders the question for a moment before answering under her influence, "I would kill anyone for the taste of your flesh, mistress."

With an evil smirk on her face, Jezebel materializes a large knife in her hands and says to her, "I want you to kill that man across the street. He makes me uncomfortable." Jezebel glares at a homeless man, sleeping in a bus stop bench.

She hands the knife to Trish who courageously says; "I'll destroy him for you. Be not afraid, mistress." With a sinister flame in her eyes, Nathan begins walking towards the bum on the other side of the street. Celestial nervously asks Crissella:

"Does she truly intend to murder that man?"

"That is what she said, is it not?"

"No, she can't! That man has done nothing wrong. She has no right to cast judgment upon him." exclaims Celestial.

Crissella holds her still as she explains, "You are no longer an angel anymore, Celestial. Let the situation play out! As demonesses, this is what we exist for."

Celestial watches in horror as Trish continues her course towards the homeless man across the street when suddenly a tall blonde haired man in a clean suit steps in front of her, blocking out the light of the street lamp.

"Pardon me, are these girls disturbing you, ma'am?"

"Get out of my way, punk, I've got something to do!" Trish yells.

The man looks at the knife and replies, "May I ask, what?"

"I'm going to get rid of that bum over there, he's making my girl uncomfortable!"

The tall man glances up at Jezebel then places his hand upon Trish's forehead, instantly knocking her unconscious.

"No, you're not," he says as she falls harmlessly onto a pile of garbage; the knife dissolves into dust upon impact with the ground.

Crissella looks toward the wall and mumbles to herself, "Oh shit."

The blonde man steps forward and says to the girls, "I thought I made it clear, not to come around here anymore. Your constant infractions of angelic decree do not bode well for your master."

Celestial suddenly realizes who the man is, and in stunned silence, she steps back as Jezebel confronts him.

"Michael, we were only playing with the mortals. You are always so tense about this kind of thing."

"Does your definition of playing include manipulation of a mortal's mind, to commit the worst sin in the eyes of our Lord? You had this man intent on killing another one of God's children, thus condemning him to an eternity of damnation in your wretched fields."

"Must you always make it sound so serious? Your God would not miss one worthless human!" Jezebel snaps back.

"No mortal is worthless in his eyes! One man is no less important than a million others." Michael glares at the sisters until he settles his eyes upon Celestial. He says to her, "You are young for a demon. I have never seen you before; your aura is unfamiliar to me."

Celestial's eyes flood with tears when she says to him, "Michael... do you not even recognize your own lover?" Michael stares into her eyes in a moment of confusion until the realization causes him to lurch back in shock.

"My Lord, have mercy! Celestial... what is this indignity that has befallen you? I heard of your expulsion from the shining city but I had no idea..."

"Oh Michael..." interrupts Celestial as she slowly steps towards him with her arms outstretched, "... there is no concept in your heart of how terribly I have missed you!" The two come together and wrap their arms around each other as they both shed tears of happiness, and sorrow.

Crissella stares at the couple in awe, and then says to Jezebel, "I must say, I am a little surprised at the outcome of this situation."

"The feeling is mutual," Jezebel says.

Celestial and Michael hold each other in silence for a moment, when he finally says to her, "I thought you were lost to me forever... I had no idea that you would be turned into one of them. I thought that you would be condemned to slavery in the burning fields, I wept for what seemed like ages thinking of you toiling away in agony."

Celestial releases her grasp from her former lover and replies, "I have been condemned to slavery, Michael...I am a slave to my fears. The absence of God within my heart is more painful than any slave driver's whip could ever be."

"Why, then do you associate with these unholy temptresses? It is not like you to commit more sins that have already been committed," asks Michael as the sisters glare at him with an expression of anger.

Celestial looks at her two sisters, then back at Michael before she says, "These temptresses are the only family I can now belong to... your God no longer accepts my presence within his kingdom. I have sinned; therefore, I have been expelled from divinity."

"Celestial, you must understand…" Michael begins to say when Celestial interrupts, "Understand what? Have I not spent eons devoting my passion and love to him… and only once do I make a mistake when he tears me from his heart and casts me into darkness? Your God has turned his back to my love, and I can never be forgiven. Let it also be known; never will I forgive him!"

Michael stands silent, knowing that he cannot argue her point. He finally says to her, "I have forgiven you. I have prayed, and I will continue to pray for your soul. Too deeply do I love you to surrender my hope of your return."

"Michael… you know that isn't possible. Once you've been exiled from Heaven, you cannot go back." she solemnly explains. Meanwhile, Crissella and Jezebel step forward and take Celestial's hand.

"Come, my sister… we must return home before we overstay our welcome here," says Crissella.

Michael glares at the two temptresses and dictates to them, "If you tempt her into becoming like you, I will make it a personal mission to end your existence! The seraphim council will no longer tolerate any more infractions made by your kind, and if these violations continue, they will send their wrath down upon you and they will smite your dark Shepard."

As Crissella walks away, pulling Celestial with her, she sneers back at Michael, "Your threats mean nothing to me, Archangel. Let us return home, sisters." Crissella growls the satanic spell to open the portal back to their forsaken home as Celestial takes a final glance into Michael's eyes, only to see tears forming on his lower lids. She turns back and enters the portal without another word spoken.

The sisters vanish from the mortal plane and Michael is left standing in the alleyway, staring into the darkness… alone.

CHAPTER FOUR

Eva's Chamber

Back in the palace, Celestial sits alone in her bedroom, pondering the event that has just taken place upon the mortal plane. Acidic rain falls over the vile kingdom while she broods. Once again in her true form, the fallen angel lets her wings fall over her body, like a blanket. She sits silently at the foot of the bed when Crissella walks in.

The door creaks closed behind her as she makes her way over to Celestial and sits down on the bed by her side. Crissella holds her hand and strokes her leathery wings to soothe her.

"Would you like to discuss this with me, sister? It seemed that you and the archangel were quite friendly in that alleyway."

"We have had previous relations. That was long ago… before I was exiled." says Celestial in a solemn tone.

"It appeared as though you two had more than just previous relations. I swear on my black heart I heard the word "lover" mentioned during the excursion." says Crissella.

"We were… in love for a time. He was separated from me when he was summoned to investigate a disturbance. I lusted for him while he was gone."

"So you have felt lust in your heart. That would explain why you were so wary on the mortal plane. It makes sense to me now." Crissella says.

"That sin was only my first. Later, when he came back, I saw him coveting a mortal female, at least that is what my jealous eyes led me to believe."

"Jealousy, that is certainly a sin to be exiled from Heaven for. The reason for your suffering is much clearer to me now," adds Crissella.

"I then tried to escape judgment, but I was caught by another archangel, Uriel. He condemned me for my sins, and in the name of God, he cast me out. Instantly, I fell… and I fell… and I fell for what seemed like an eternity in itself until I landed here."

Crissella strokes Celestial's silky hair and pulls her head against her chest to say, "Do not let remorse tear you apart. What happened cannot be reversed, but because of it, you have gained a new family, and a new home that accepts you, imperfections and all. Living here is not as bad as some lesser minds portray, but only because you were fortunate enough to become one of us."

Celestial grows a blank stare towards the ground in reaction to the words that were said by her sister. Slowly she stands up from the bed and walks away from Crissella, who says, "What is the matter, sister?"

"I remember, all too well… because of you, I was transformed into this creature, this shadow of an angel. You dare say I was blessed with fortune to become what I am!"

Crissella cautiously stands up and with a stern look in her eyes; she says to her sister, "Why do you become angered at yourself so suddenly? Jezebel and I made you a god among slaves in this land; you should be grateful!"

With fire burning in her eyes, Celestial yells, "You raped me! The most divine members of an angel's body were torn from my back by your hands, and you watched me bleed until I became one of you!"

Fiercely challenging the argument, Crissella storms forward and growls, "Have you no concept of how lucky you are to be one of us? Would you rather have been made a slave, so that you may be whipped and degraded for eternity? I was mortal like every other human that walks the Earth until I passed on to this world. I was destined to be a slave like every other petty sinner who agonizes out there. I too was raped, but by the hands of one of Satan's guards, thus transforming me into the fierce creature I am now!"

The fire in Celestial's eyes burns out, when she sympathetically says, "I had no idea, Crissella. I apologize if I let my anger get the better of me."

Crissella's eyes swell with tears, having remembered the suffering that has long passed, "No, you are right to be angry. I know too well what it means to hate yourself for your mistakes. I learned long ago that I could not change the course of my life or the mistakes that I made, but also I learned to not let my hatred tear me apart from within. I have come to accept myself for what I am, not who I used to be." Crissella turns away and walks over to the stone dresser against the wall.

"It has been far too long since I've felt the kind of love that you and Michael shared with each other. My soul is driven by lust and the longing of my flesh. I crave physical pleasure like children crave candy, yet I can never truly satisfy my desire. That is my curse, Celestial… and now it is yours as well."

A knock at the door interrupts the tense emotion in the room as the imp, Sorthen, peers his ragged head from the hallway.

"I hate to interrupt you, ladies, if you're… doing something…"

"What lost wager has sent you here, maggot?" Sneers Crissella.

"I've come to tell you that mistress Eva would like to speak with you." informs the imp.

"Eva? For what purpose does that bitch request our presence?"

"She didn't say. She just sent me to fetch you sultry temptresses, in exchange for a reward." Sorthen chuckles.

Crissella glances at Celestial as she motions for her to follow him. The disfigured little imp leads the two demonesses to the bedchamber where the queen of Hell resides. Passing through grand halls, lit by torches, Celestial curiously looks around at all of the foreboding sculptures carved into the walls. The figures that represent the great battles of Earth are actually the condemned souls of sinners who are trapped inside the marble. Their eyes follow the girls while moaning in pain, as they walk down the hall towards the richly decorated double doors of Eva's chamber. Two large statues of the infamous Minotaur stand guard on each side of the entrance; they stand nearly twenty feet tall and they each grasp a mighty ax in its hands.

The imp, Sorthen pulls open the door and invites the girls into the room. Eva's chamber is large, with blood-red drapery hanging from the ceiling. A wide, raised bed, sits in the middle of the room. The sisters look around in awe until Crissella spies the beaten lump in the corner that is Jezebel. Her body is bruised and covered in fresh slash marks, made by a multi-tail whip and her wings are cut and bleeding. She holds her legs against her chest as she trembles in shock. With tears of pain in her eyes, she looks up at Crissella.

"Jezebel…" Crissella says in angst.

A clanking noise from the rear of the room draws the girl's attention to a voluptuous, red-haired woman placing a multi-tailed whip into its rack upon the wall.

The woman says to the girls, "Well, it seems the troublesome brats have finally arrived." She turns around to face the girls with a pair of flaming red eyes that burn brighter than the hottest torch in the hall. The woman is stunningly beautiful, almost angelic, yet a chilling aura of evil surrounds her. Anything she touches frosts over with ice and her voice travels with a piercing resonance. Her flowing dress glimmers in the torchlight as she strides towards the sisters.

"What have you done to my sister, evil bitch?" Growls Crissella.

"Oh, I've simply taught her the error of her ways, seeing how she's managed to get the entire angelic community infuriated at us, it was a fitting punishment for that pathetic creature!"

Sorthen hobbles over to Eva with a sprightly gimp and says to her, "I've done what you commanded my queen. I brought her sisters here. Shall I be rewarded now, Mistress?"

Eva looks down at the imp with a sinister expression of accolade and says to him, "Of course, Sorthen. You know I'm a madam of my word." With the snap of her fingers, Eva instantly transforms Sorthen into a wriggling maggot on the floor. She reaches down and picks him up by her two fingers.

"We always said he was a maggot anyway, so it's only fitting that he spend the rest of his days as one. Although his day won't be very long I'm afraid." Eva walks over to a shelf on the wall where she takes the lid off of a jar filled with fire ants. Their mandibles are extremely large in comparison with a regular ant found on Earth. Eva tosses the wriggling maggot into the jar to let the ants devour the helpless creature alive. She puts the lid back on the jar and walks back over to the sisters.

"Well, he's always wanted to feel the pleasures of excruciating pain... His wish has been granted."

Crissella and Celestial look at each other in uneasy shock, and then Crissella says to Eva, "Why have you summoned us? Do you wish to beat us as well, like you beat my sister?"

Eva smirks at the girl and steps closer to her saying, "Well actually..." Eva quickly swings her arm and slaps Crissella across the face, knocking her to the ground, "... that's exactly why I summoned you!" She stands over the fallen Crissella and continues saying, "As sisters, you must share the punishment for one's action! You are the most pathetic excuses for demons in this land, you show no worth to this kingdom and if I had my way, I would destroy you both right now. Since my King demands you stay alive for his personal pleasure, I won't kill you!" Eva violently kicks Crissella in the stomach, knocking the wind out of her. She rolls around on the floor coughing and gasping for air.

"But I can still make you wish for death," she growls with another brutal kick.

Celestial steps back in shock at the violence occurring before her eyes, then Eva quickly says to her, "Where do you think you're going, honey? I have some for you as well."

"Why do you punish them like this? They don't deserve this kind of treatment from someone like you!" spouts Celestial.

Eva squints her eyes at the defiant demoness then states, "Are you questioning me? You must enjoy pain very much... angel trash!" Eva steps over Crissella and confronts Celestial eye to eye.

Instead of giving in to fear, Celestial stands her ground and defiantly stares the evil Queen in the eyes. The two women stay there for a moment staring each other down when Eva grins and says to Celestial:

"You're a brave soul, angel. Have you no fear of me?"

"I have no fear of any creature that is lesser than I. Release my sisters, now!"

Eva steps back in astonishment from the act of righteousness when she responds, "Your tone is pleasing. You are direct and show much passion for your fellow minions. You'll take no shit from anyone! If only we had more creatures like you... we would be the dominant power in this universe and your former angel friends would bow to us!"

Eva walks around the room looking at the two sisters, who are writhing in pain on the floor and then looks back at Celestial.

"Take your sisters and return to your chamber. They have suffered enough punishment, for now."

Celestial pulls Crissella up from the floor, and then they walk over to Jezebel who is trembling from the agony inflicted upon her. The sisters gently grab Jezebel and hold her up with her arms over each other's shoulder. As the trio walks out of the door, Eva suddenly says:

"Oh, and boys... you may have your fun with my girls." Her wicked grin is the last thing the sisters see of Eva before the doors slam closed.

Celestial looks at Crissella in confusion and asks, "What did she mean by that?" Crissella shrugs her shoulders when suddenly the two Minotaur statues turn and look at the sisters. Their eyes burst with red flame as they drag their stone feet from their pedestals.

"Hello, ladies! It's time for some fun!" the closest Minotaur says with an evil cackle. The creatures slap their ax handles against their palms as they thunder closer to the sisters.

Crissella urgently says to Celestial, "Run… with much haste!" With a quick burst of energy, Crissella yanks the weakened Jezebel up into her arms and takes off running. Celestial quickly follows.

"Get back here! Grab the bitches!" Shouts the Minotaur as they both pursue the fleeing sisters. With every step, a crater is left in the marble floor and the hall shakes like thunder.

As Celestial runs, she glances at the torches that light the hallway and suddenly stops in her tracks. She yells to Crissella who still carries their sister in her arms, "Get her away from here! I will handle these creatures!" She turns to face the charging bulls when Crissella yells to her:

"Have you lost your mind? They'll rip you apart!"

"Trust me, I have faith within my heart." Without argument, Crissella continues running out of the hallway while Celestial stares down the approaching demons. She says to herself:

"Now would appear to be a good time to release these wings of mine!" With a rush of adrenaline coursing through her body, Celestial unfolds her black wings until the ends point toward the sky. The height of the wings from base to tip is nearly double her height, as they tower over Celestial's sensuous body. She begins flapping them as hard as she can until she is raised into the air. Each stroke kicks up a cloud of dust and soot as Celestial hovers patiently.

Celestial continues to stare down the beasts that shout at her, "You're ours now, little girl! I've got something for you that'll tear you in half!"

"You're right… it is time to play!" Celestial utters to herself as she rapidly lunges forward towards the bull demons. Surprised by her action, the demons stop running soon enough for Celestial to dash between them, she then ends up hovering above them on the other side of the hallway. She quickly throws herself toward one of the torches on the wall and rips it from its holder.

With a speed that leaves the lumbering beasts no time to react, Celestial flies between them once again as she smacks them both in their faces with the flaming torch. The burning embers fly from their cheeks as the right-hand bull yells:

"You treacherous wench! I will grind your bones to dust for that!" With a mighty swing of his stone ax, the Minotaur attempts to hit

Celestial as she flies away, but instead smashes his weapon into the wall, gouging a large hole from the slab of rock. Debris explodes in every direction as he tears his ax out of the limestone wall, and Celestial returns to smack him in the face once more with the flaming torch.

"It would appear that you missed! Perhaps your ax is too big for your brain!" Celestial Taunts.

The second Minotaur lowers his ax and reaches into a pouch on the side of his belt; with lightning speed, he flings three large spinning blades at the unsuspecting demoness."

"Shit!" she yells, as she acrobatically dodges the projectiles, which lodge into the wall behind her.

Angrily Celestial yells at the Minotaur, "I don't appreciate demons throwing weapons at me!" She hurls the flaming torch at the offending Minotaur, only to have it pierce through his left eye.

"Aaaaarrrrrgggghhhhhh!" screams the beast as he lunges back from the pain. Celestial flies toward him and causes him to blindly swing his ax at her. He smashes it into the ground and then through the walls as he furiously attempts to hit the elusive demoness. Finally, Celestial flies up behind the first Minotaur and perches herself on his back.

"What are you doing? Get off of me, you whore!" Unbeknownst to the Minotaur, his brother sees only Celestial before him, and so he swings his ax at the demoness.

"Noooooooo!" The demon screams, as his brother's ax, comes down upon his head, splitting and cracking him down the center of his body. Celestial quickly flies off as the demon crumbles into a pile of rock, which instantly turns to dust and blows throughout the hallway.

The remaining Minotaur continues to blindly swing his ax into every wall and fixture he can hit, hoping that he takes Celestial with it. She, however, has flown back up to where the spinning blades have been lodged into the wall. Celestial struggles to pull the blades out, but finally, she frees one. The curved blade almost forms a disk shape that can easily fly through the air.

Celestial yells out to the Minotaur, "Hey maggot, I'm up here!" The semi blinded Minotaur looks up at her and lets out a mighty roar that shakes the hall.

Celestial says to him, "Here's a present, courtesy of my sisters!" as she springs off of the wall and lunges directly at him with incredible speed, the beast reels his arm back in preparation to swing his massive ax. As he hurls it forward, Celestial winds her arm back to throw the blade at the beast's neck. She releases the blade at a blinding velocity as she twists her body to the side, narrowly escaping the ax's edge. The spinning blade slices clean through the Minotaur's throat, lodging itself once again into the wall on the other side. The momentum of the beast's ax tears it from his grasp and sends it smashing into the opposite wall, shattering into millions of pieces.

Celestial rolls to a stop on the ground and looks back to see the Minotaur standing absolutely still.   The fires that burn in his eyes slowly expire as the creeping resonance of rock sliding against rock pierces the air.   The beast's head slides slowly across its neck and eventually tumbles to the ground, shattering into pieces that fade to dust. The rest of his body crumbles like a jagged cliff and blows away throughout the hall.

With a sigh of relief, Celestial takes a much-needed rest upon the ground, relaxing from the adrenaline rush of surviving the intense ordeal.

"What a couple of stiffs," she laughs.

CHAPTER FIVE

Crissellas Walk

Having brought her wounded sister to rest in their bedchamber, Crissella paces outside of the door, pondering the violent confrontation that has just taken place.

"That bitch tried to kill us, unbelievable… she will pay dearly for this outrage, I swear upon my soul! She has no courage to kill us with her own hands, that cowardly whore!"

Crissella walks away down the hall until she comes to a window that looks over the mountain ranges. Amidst the smoldering rock and the flowing rivers of lava that snake throughout the land, Crissella lays eyes upon a peculiar travel party, making its way into the canyon.

"Eva… where is that witch heading off to? There is a bone that I wish to pick with you… all of them," Crissella mutters as she turns to walk down the hall. Winding through the grimy passages and past the moaning artwork that lines the walls, Crissella closes in on the main gate as she angrily storms down the foreboding hallway.

Suddenly as Crissella rounds a corner, she runs into her master, Satan, who is casually dressed in his mortal appearance.

"Oh… Master… I apologize for my insolence, I did not see you there," Crissella pleads with a bowed head.

Satan wipes off his suit in a disgusted manner and then says, "Where do you think you're going, my dear? You seemed to be in somewhat of a hurry."

"There is something I wish to take care of, it is… important."

Satan's eyes glow red as he growls, "Is it so important that you run into me with such disrespect!"

Crissella falls to her knees with her hands clenched as she grovels,

"Please master, I apologize for my disrespectfulness."

"That's right… fall to your knees, slave. That is the only position you are good at performing!" Satan looks around to see if anyone is watching them, when he finally says, "Get up!   I desire some company… and you just volunteered."

Satan grabs Crissella by the arms and pulls her to her feet and then drags her down the hall towards his bedchamber. Crissella wants to plea against their sexual pairing but she knows that he'll only be angered more.

"I'm feeling aroused right now and you're going to help satisfy my desire!" Satan says as he flings open the door to his bedchamber. Dragging Crissella by the arm, Satan tosses her on the bed, where he pins her down between the pillows.

Crissella pants in fear at what her master might do, but that fear soon becomes terror when Satan morphs into his true demonic self. Looking around the all too familiar room, Crissella's brow glazes over with sweat, as she eyes the multiple implements of pain and pleasure that hang upon the wall. Unable to stare directly at the horrendous face of her master, Crissella turns her head to the side as the lord of darkness says to her…

"That's a good little slave girl! You always know your place… beneath me! I must say that you come in handy when my Queen isn't around! She seems to have disappeared somewhere, and no one seems to know where."

With his dripping snake-like tongue, Satan licks the side of Crissella's face leaving a trail of foul-smelling slime across her cheek. Now in tears, the vulnerable temptress utters to her overpowering master…

"I know… where Eva is… master."

He pulls his explorative tongue back inside his mouth and responds…

"What? By what do you mean you know where she is?"

"She's heading towards the canyon master.   I saw her myself through the window." Sharply, Satan sits up and says to himself…

"Why… would she go there, especially now?"

After a moment of hesitation, he jumps off of the bed and storms out of his chamber leaving Crissella alone on top of the sweat-soaked sheets. The nearly violated demoness breaks down into tears from the pent up fear that filled her body. Every memory that she has ever had with her master flashes through her mind, tormenting her even more, as she rolls to her side to sob her pain away.

***

Entering the chilled throne room, Satan shouts to his various guards and slaves…

"Who here has seen my Queen?"

The guards look around at each other in confusion when from behind Eva's voice speaks out, "Are you looking for me, lover? I am here!" Satan approaches his dark Queen in frustration to inquiry her trip.

"It has come to my attention that you took a trip to the black canyons. Tell me, Eva, for what purpose did you go there?"

"Oh no, honey, you don't need to get all huffy about it. I was just taking a little stroll through the mortal plane… that's all."

"You know damn well the seriousness of the situation on the mortal plane! Heaven's army will not hesitate to invade my kingdom for these infractions!"

"Since when did you become such a sniveling little baby, Lucifer? I thought you were…" Satan angrily interrupts Eva's statement.

"Never again will you utter that name to me! I am the Lord of darkness, the Shepard of lost souls… I am the harvester of hatred, and you will refer to me as such!"

"You have yet to give me a reason as to why you should deserve such titles!" A tense silence floods the air as Satan's anger rages throughout his every muscle at the brutal statement made by his only love. The couple stands and stares at each other in hateful silence until Satan finally backs down.

Satan turns and thunders away down the hallway towards a dark retreat. Along the way, the dark lord slugs the guards who stand at the entrance in fury, knocking them both to the ground where their broken bodies twitch and squirm.

Eva continues to stare in malice as her angered husband storms away from her. A sinister smirk grows upon her face as she mutters to herself…

"It's only a matter of time, my lord… you won't have to worry about this power struggle anymore."

***

* * *

Crissella has since fled her master's chambers and is now sneaking down a cold and wet passageway within the depths of the palace, where she is lost in reflection. She constantly struggles with the thoughts of what her life would have been, had she not been found by Satan's guards. Slavery comes in many forms, and Crissella quickly realizes that she could not win in any situation.

Watching the endless columns of brimstone drift by, she finally enters a cavernous room full of chained up slaves and their merciless captors. The only light filtering into the room comes from scattered torches upon the walls and the glowing eyes of the demon slave drivers. The chained slaves, who are visibly starved, are forced to sit on the floor mere feet from a row of bountiful food and drinks.

Crissella walks tenderly down the central aisle where the food rests and looks at each of the suffering souls upon the floor. She glances at a dark-haired girl who looks up at her in tears; Crissella stares in sympathy at the girl, who closely resembles herself.

Crissella approaches the head slave master in the center of the room with merciful eyes. He is a horned beast, clad in heavy armor and a helmet that allows only his flaming eyes to be seen. As Crissella approaches, he greets the demoness with a nod.

"Mistress," he states, "Is there any way I could be of service to you, milady?"

"Tell me, slave driver, do you allow any of these slaves to eat… even a small morsel?" Crissella asks.

"Ha… of course not, Mistress; these maggots do not deserve to eat. They are the worst of all gluttons who ate more than their fair share of food during their worthless lives. Now they, at last, know the pain of having to starve, and we intend to keep it that way."

"Have you no sense of charity in your black heart?" she says.

"Charity? Their lack of charity is what brought these creatures to us in the first place. Do not insult me by comparing me to mortals!" growls the slave driver.

Crissella looks around at the emaciated souls who suffer great physical pain from their lack of food. The empathetic temptress walks toward a large plate of food near the dark-haired woman, while the headmaster watches in confusion. Crissella kneels down to grab a piece of bread from the plate and then tenderly hands it to the girl, whose eyes light up with immeasurable joy.

"Here you go, sweetheart… savor every bite." Crissella says to the overjoyed woman. She hands out more pieces of food to other slaves until the head slave driver shouts out…

"What in all of Hell do you think you're doing? Drop that food right now, maggots!" Several demons close in on the feasting slaves and lash them with their multi-tailed whips. In fury, Crissella stands up and glares at the headmaster with burning eyes.

"Leave them alone, foul beast! They have done nothing to deserve this kind of treatment from scum like you!"

"This is Hell, bitch! They deserve every moment of pain and suffering that befalls them!" The headmaster shouts at Crissella as the other two demons surround her with their whips in hand. She scans the scene and sizes up each opponent, and then she says to the demonic trio…

"Don't… even… dare!" The demon behind Crissella let's out a shout of rage as it suddenly charges towards her. Crissella waits for the charging beast to get closer when suddenly she elegantly shoves her leg backward and then up; her razor sharp claws pierce straight through the creature's jugular causing black blood to gush from the wound. The second demon in front quickly charges Crissella, but she drags the impaled demon around from behind her and kicks him towards his fellow slave driver, impaling him with his jagged horns; they both fall to the ground and crumble into dust.

Crissella stares down the headmaster who can't believe what he's just seen. The demon roars in anger then says to Crissella…

"I will make you pay for your insolence, temptress whore! You will join these slaves to suffer with them for the rest of eternity!"

"Try your hardest, beast!" Crissella stands defiantly as the large demon storms toward her with his sword drawn. The beast fiercely swings his blade, but Crissella jumps and flips over his head, landing behind him. Crissella grabs hold of the demon's horns, and with a single violent twist, she breaks his neck like a piece of driftwood. The creature drops to the floor and dissipates into the air, while Crissella picks up his sword and says to the slaves…

"You have been blessed with freedom, feast until your heart is content." With the sword in hand Crissella swings and breaks the chain that holds all of the slaves together; they let out a cheer of joy and dive into the food that lays before them. Crissella quietly backs away and turns toward the main door out of the chamber. Just as she reaches for the handle to open the door, the dark-haired woman puts her hand upon her right shoulder and says…

"Mistress… I can't thank you enough for what you've done. I never would have thought that angels could exist in Hell!" Crissella stares in amazement at the act of compassion; her eyes light up with a kind of fire that is not like Hellfire, it is brighter and burns with a blue radiance. Crissella grins as she turns and says to the slave girl…

"You are most welcome, child. I did only what I could… which is more than what has been done for me."

To Crissella's surprise, the woman steps forward and wraps her arms around her in a warm hug. Crissella is stunned at the act for a second, but she timidly returns the hug to the woman. Stepping back from Crissella, the dark haired slave says…

"Thank you… again! You have no idea how much I appreciate this!" The woman then returns to the group to fill her stomach. With a spark of warmth in her heart, Crissella leaves the chamber and continues her walk.

***

Within the depths of the unholy palace, Satan saunters among a barren ground in a hidden room. He scans the width of the empty garden and opens his palm, where three seeds lie. He rubs the seeds with his finger and says to himself:

"Please father, bear me fruit that I may eat for my own."

He casts the seeds into the dry soil and stands patiently for a sprout. Moments pass when small stalks emerge from the ground where the seeds were cast. Satan kneels down to witness the growth of the plants, but as he picks an immature fruit from the stalk, it crumbles to dust in his palm. The stalks that were green for a blink of an eye quickly dry up and wither. Satan falls to his knees in angst and buries his head in the soil, silently weeping to himself.

CHAPTER SIX

A Sister's Vow

In the darkness of the bedchamber, Crissella sits by her wounded sister, who sleeps silently under the covers. The concerned sister tenderly strokes Jezebel's head in comfort while she ponders the trauma that has befallen her. She rubs a cloth, damp with healing ointments, across Jezebel's wounds while her wings drape over the edge of the bed.

Leaning down to whisper into her ear, Crissella says, "I will avenge you, my sister... by any means possible. Eva will suffer terribly for what she's done to you." She kisses Jezebel on the cheek when suddenly Celestial limps into the room.

"What happened to you?" Crissella asks with concern.

"Eva might need a couple of new statues to guard her door," smirks Celestial. Crissella stands up from the bed and marched over to her.

"You're hurt. Did they..."

"No, I landed too harshly. I am not quite accustomed to my wings as of yet, and I am obviously not familiar with the halls in this palace!" Chuckles Celestial.

"Come and lie down next to Jezebel. Give yourself a rest, you could use one." Crissella paces around the room in anger as Celestial awkwardly crawls into her side of the bed. She looks over at her quietly sleeping sister, and then she utters:

"Is she alright?"

"She'll be fine. She needs time to rest and regenerate, her wounds will heal soon." Crissella replies. She walks over to her dresser and slams her palm down in anger. She looks into the mirror on the wall and says:

"I vow on this day, I will have my revenge on the Bitch Queen who did this! The legend of my vengeance will spread throughout this plane and the next! Those who seek to challenge me will be paralyzed with fear before they raise a single weapon against me."

"You must realize, sister, a creature like Eva will receive threefold what she gives. It is a universal law that all spirits obey, whether they realize it or not." Informs Celestial as she nurses her sore leg.

"Your God in Heaven knows she will receive it! She will receive more than her heart is aware of!" Crissella sneers as she pushes away from her dresser.

***

Meanwhile in the black chamber of the Lord of Darkness, Satan, in his mortal guise, converses with his wicked Queen concerning the recent attack by the Minotaur demons.

"That fallen angel doesn't seem trustworthy enough to keep around here. She's far too rebellious and righteous to be an effective minion of mine!"

"She is the first soul who has ever stood up against me in outright defiance! Personally... I was pleased by her attitude, but her angelic heritage makes her a threat to our kingdom." Says Eva. She sits on the bed and stares at the grotesque paintings of pain and suffering that hang upon the wall while holding a finger to her chin, deep in thought.

Standing next to her, Satan suggests to his queen, "Her threat is much greater now that the angelic community is preparing to raze my kingdom to the ground! They'll look for any excuse to invade so that they can destroy us. All she has to do is slip up once, and Armageddon will rain down upon this land."

"I say let them invade. We will destroy them all if they dare come here!" Eva says with a sinister glare on her face

"That's why I love you so much. You always find a way to justify destruction!" Satan replies as he wraps his cold arms around her waist. The evil couple kisses and fondles each other for a moment when Satan asks, "What should we do about the "fallen one"?"

"I have something special planned for her," Eva answers with a menacing chuckle.

***

* * *

Several hours later, Crissella and Celestial have once again taken human forms and have traveled onto the mortal plane where they sit together in a small coffee house in Pennsylvania. The sisters are dressed so that they don't draw attention to themselves from any angelic eyes. Black overcoats and gloves blend in with the winter-laden mortals that sit around them.

"Is it safe for us to even be here?" asks Celestial as she cautiously looks around.

"Angelic decree does not state anything about our kind traveling to the mortal plane. It only speaks against our interference with mortal lives."

"And what if they interfere with us?" Celestial inquires.

"They won't. I've put a spell on us that makes you and I "socially invisible". They have no desire whatsoever to come over and talk to us." Crissella looks around the table for something to play with, and then finally she rips open a sugar packet and pours the entire contents into her mouth. With a jolt from the ensuing sugar rush, she smiles at Celestial.

"You… have issues." She comments.

Crissella licks her lips before adding, "Imagine for a moment. How many sweet foods do we have down there? The supply of Twinkies and cookies has been running dry for quite some time." Crissella says with a grin. Celestial can only giggle in agreement as she realizes that her sister has a point. The demoness looks around at the people in the coffee house, watching them interact with each other as if the outside world doesn't even exist.

"I vote to leave this place… these people aren't the kind I like to be around." The Sisters stand up and walk out onto the snow-covered sidewalk.   While walking down the sidewalk, Jezebel suddenly appears from behind the corner of a blue building.

"You're awake! Do you feel any better?" Crissella asks.

"I feel quite well, in fact! I needed a rest, I haven't had one in such a long time," explains Jezebel.

"I am pleased to see you feeling better, sister. I took care of those Minotaurs while you were out." gloats Celestial.

"Really? You have more tenacity then most demons would credit you for." Jezebel asks.

"Ashes to ashes, dust to dust," she replied.

"Excellent, my sister!" Jezebel gives her a high-five in praise. The girls turn and continue walking, looking at the snowy scenery.

"I wish home could be as beautiful as this, especially considering how cold it is inside the palace," states Crissella as she drags her finger through a pile of snow on a low window ledge.

"Heaven was beautiful like this, except it wasn't cold." Celestial describes as she looks toward the sky.

"So, Celestial… what is Heaven like?" Crissella asks with a somber tone of voice. Surprised by her sudden question, Celestial begins explaining Heaven with vivid detail.

"Well, the city is built around an obelisk of light. The buildings are laced in silver and jade and glimmer with God's love. His essence resides in a golden palace that stands in the center of the city; from which the obelisk stands. Heaven is very warm, though not like Hell, it is warm with love and happiness which floods through your body at every moment of every day."

"Wow, it seems so pleasant! I wish I could say that I've seen it…" Jezebel utters.

"Don't wrap yourself up in the beauty. It seems that Heaven has a revolving door policy, where they will throw you out as soon as you feel an emotion that doesn't agree with their way of thinking." Celestial says in an aggravated manner.

"They would 'love' me in that case," Crissella quips. They continue walking for a moment when she follows up with, "May I ask how you and Michael met each other?"

"Oh, I can't quite recall how long ago it was, but…" Celestial giggles suddenly then continue, "… actually I kind of whapped him in the face with my wing." Crissella and Jezebel stop walking and look back at Celestial in surprise.

"It wasn't on purpose! It was an accident, kind of." Informs Celestial. "He was walking around a corner while I wasn't paying attention. I was explaining something to one of my friends when I got really excited and opened my wings, thereby whapping him in the face. The rest of the story explains itself."

"Now that is funny! When I desire to meet the man of my dreams, I now know to smack him in the face and say how sorry I am!" Jezebel says with a chortle. The girls chuckle together before continuing their stroll down the sidewalk.

"Do you suppose that Eva will come after us for destroying her precious statues?" asks Jezebel in a cynical manner.

"It doesn't matter if she does! We will be waiting for her! I have already formulated a plan on how we will exact our revenge." snorts

Crissella.

As the sisters walk around the corner, they stumble upon a car accident that has just occurred in the intersection. One of the vehicles is flipped onto its roof while the other vehicle is smashed into a telephone pole. With much interest, the sisters run to get a closer look at the devastation.

"Ooh, I love destruction! The panic in the crowd's eyes... it invigorates me in ways that dare not speak their name!" shouts Crissella.

Celestial looks over the accident scene to see if anyone has been hurt or not. Looking towards the overturned car, she sees an old homeless woman helping the people out of the vehicle and is stunned by what she sees. Staring in confusion Celestial tries to understand what her eyes are witnessing.

Celestial continues to be amazed while watching the woman rescue the trapped family. The moment she pulls them to the side of the street, a driver who hasn't been paying attention plows into the side of the overturned car, pushing it further down the street. The crowd gasps in shock as they witness the new collision and several Samaritans run to help the driver in the new car.

Standing in shock Crissella and Jezebel looks at each other in amazement, then back at Celestial. Crissella says to her:

"Did you see that? If that woman wasn't there to help those people..."

"I know... there is something special about her. We should leave, before the watchful eyes of an archangel assumes we did this." Implies Celestial as she walks away from the scene.

"That idea is sound to me! Let's get out of here while we can." Jezebel adds as she follows her sisters.

The sisters briskly stride away from the accident scene, nervously looking around for the eyes of a prying angel. Police cars and emergency vehicles tear around the corner with their sirens blaring passing the girls on their way to the collision.

Crissella walks up closer to Celestial and says, "So, you said that lady was special... what did you mean by that?"

Celestial continues looking around as she replies, "I could see her aura, and it was different than that of any mortal's I have seen."

"How was it different?" asks Jezebel.

"She had the aura of an angel, yet she had no wings. She couldn't simply have been in the guise of a mortal, not with an aura like that! I can not be sure but there may be another level of the angelic hierarchy that I was not aware of."

"How is it possible that you wouldn't know of another level?" inquires Jezebel.

"I was part of, what I thought was, the bottom level of the hierarchy and so I didn't have access to as much knowledge as the higher ranked angels. There are certain privileges that come with status, in Heaven."

The girls turn another corner and briskly walk towards an alleyway to the right when suddenly two muscular men in street clothes step out and confront them.

"Hi, there girls… it's nice meeting you here." One of them says with a sinister smirk upon his face.

The sisters stop in panic as they take notice of the men's eyes glowing bright with hellfire. Celestial quickly asks, "What do you want with us?"

"The master sent us to deliver a message to you, "fallen one"!" The second man growls. Simultaneously, the two men roar in anger, bearing their fangs, as their faces and body violently distort into their demonic selves. Their black wings rip through their clothes and rows of horns grow out from their skulls. The people standing around on the streets scream in terror and run for their lives, some unknowingly run through the streets only to be hit and killed by the traffic that still flows through the city.

The sisters step back out of range of the two demons as they wield their hell-borne weapons, the one demon with a spiked mace and the other with a burning sword.

"Run!" Yells Celestial as she jumps out of the way of the swinging mace, letting it smash into the concrete. The sisters flee in panic while the demons run after them, cutting down innocent people who step in their way. The demon with the mace smashes one man's skull into a department store window, killing him instantly. The man never saw the creatures coming.

The sisters bolt across the busy streets, narrowly avoiding traffic. The demons cut across the street in pursuit when a car slams on its brakes and stops mere inches from the mace-wielding demon. Furiously, the creature lets out a mighty roar as he raises his weapon and plunges it down into the hood of the old car, flipping it end over end until it falls onto another car that as just entered the intersection. Chunks of metal and glass explode across the city block from the collision.

The demons continue their pursuit as they unfold their wings and take flight after the sisters. Crissella looks back to see the creatures closing in on them, she then yells to her sisters:

"We must find an alleyway somewhere! It will buy us some time so that we can open a portal back!"

Jezebel spies an alleyway several blocks away shouting, "There's one, hurry!" The sisters run faster in the hopes that they'll reach the alleyway before the demons catch them, however Celestial looks back and sees the demon with the flaming sword ascending in preparation to strike.

"Watch out, he's coming down!" She yells as the demon lunges downward with his sword above his head. The sisters make it to the alleyway and Crissella and Jezebel dive into it, while Celestial is forced to leap out of the way as they demon slams into the ground, bringing his sword down with such force, it ruptures the asphalt straight across to the other side of the street. Cars launch off of the cracked pavement and crash into the sidewalk, piling up vehicles one after another, virtually blocking the alleyway. Celestial spies her sisters on the other side as they run inside of a building. The demons look over at her as she jumps up and runs into the opposing alleyway; they quickly give chase.

Celestial reverts to her demonic state in preparation to fly out of the alleyway but she looks up only to see a mess of telephone wires and high voltage lines that prevent her from escaping. She swiftly turns around to see the two demons standing at the entrance of the alleyway, breathing heavily from chasing her and her sisters.

"It's the end of the line, sweetheart. Get ready to meet oblivion, angel bitch!" growls the sword-wielding demon.

Celestial stands in a hostile posture, bearing her fangs and claws as she growls, "Come and take me!" She lets out a guttural roar in defiance as the large demons walk closer to her. They lift their weapons to deliver their death blow when suddenly a fully armor clad Michael yells in rage from behind as he swings his glowing sword and slices through the torso of the mace-wielding demon. The unholy creature's black blood splatters across the walls of the alleyway as both pieces of his body falls to the ground and dissolves into nothingness.

"Stay away from her, unholy beast!" yells Michael as he swings his sword at the remaining demon, which holds up his evil sword to block Michael's swing. The opposing blades clash in a brilliant burst of positive and negative energy. The two warriors parry and collide their swords together as they try to best each other. Michael is able to distract the demon with a false swing and cuts the creature's arm. In a fit of rage, the beast violently swings at Michael, knocking him backward from the power behind his thrust.

Celestial watches in apprehension as her former lover courageously fights the demon, she then looks over at a pile of garbage in the corner and sees a rusty water pipe amongst it. She grabs it and angrily strides over to the demon.

"I don't appreciate demons trying to kill me!" She swings the pipe at the back of the creature's knees and brings him to the ground. With a brutal swing, Michael decapitates the evil beast with lightning speed. The demon's boiling blood gushes from its neck as the body falls forward and evaporates from existence.

Michael staggers around for a moment as he tries to catch his breath. Celestial looks up at him on the brink of crying and says, "Oh, Michael… never would I have thought…" She bursts into tears as she runs over and wraps her arms around him. He drops his sword and returns the loving embrace while he too sheds tears of happiness. The two winged beings, both from opposite ends of the universe, stand in joyous silence in the dark alleyway.

Several minutes pass by before Michael is able to speak to his forsaken love, "I was overseeing the accident back there when I saw you girls walking away. I followed you for a while until the demons gave chase."

"I was so frightened, Michael! I almost thought I was going to be taken from existence! I never would have imagined that you would be the one to find me." Cries Celestial as she clenches tighter onto Michael's Heavenly Armor.

"I know, Celestial. I would do anything within my power to keep you out of harm's way, even if it meant defying my lord." Michael responds.

"No, Michael, do not speak like that! I lost my divinity over my fear of losing you, don't throw yours away because of me."

Suddenly the couple hears a male voice shouting out from the street, "Michael, where are you?"

"Oh no, Uriel!" Michael glances in the direction of the voice and then looks back at Celestial.

"You must hide somewhere! He can not see you here or you will be persecuted by the seraphim."

"I'll open a portal home…"

"No you must not go back!" urges Michael.

"Why not, it's my home now!" shouts Celestial as she pulls away from Michael.

Hesitantly Michael explains to her, "Dire events are soon to befall the forsaken land! The seraphim council will view this assault as a direct attack on Heaven itself. They are finished looking the other way for the sake of peace!"

Celestial glowers in confusion as she asks, "What will they do?"

"Michael, where are you? Are you alright?" Uriel shouts once again. Michael impatiently tells Celestial, "Just hide here until nightfall, I will find you and explain everything!"

"Where can I hide?" asks Celestial. Michael aims his hand towards the power lines above and temporarily suspends the electricity from moving through them.

"Hide up there. There is a large ventilation shaft that you can stay in tonight. I must go." replies Michael.

Celestial gives him a quick kiss on the lips saying, "Thank you, Michael," then proceeds to climb the wall towards the roof of the building. As she climbs, she can hear Michael meeting with his brother.

"Uriel, I'm here."

"There you are, brother, I was beginning to worry about you," explains Uriel, who also is in a mortal guise, "What in the Lord's name happened down here?"

"Demons. There were two warriors wielding weapons forged from Hellfire. They devastated this city, but I know not their reason for doing so."

"Well, it doesn't matter what their reason was; the seraphim council will not tolerate this insubordination to go unpunished. This was a very deadly act, Michael, and unfortunately, for those who bow to the dark lord, it will be their last. Come, we must return to the shining city to hear the council's decision in this matter." Uriel informs Michael as he opens a portal to the Holy Land, they briskly enter and are whisked from the mortal plane.

On the roof of the building, Celestial swallows hard with unease as she rests her head against the ledge. Quietly, she stands up and walks towards the ventilation shaft where she will wait for the rest of the day. Climbing inside, Celestial wraps her wings around her cold body and prepares to relax until nightfall.

CHAPTER SEVEN

The Coming of the Storm

Within the Golden palace of God's dwelling, Michael and Uriel stand outside of the chamber, in wait for their next actions.

"Should the council decide to invade, will they destroy everything?" Michael asks in a solemn manner.

"The Seraphim will seek the eradication of all evil in the darkness, mortal sinners and the like," replies Uriel in an equally solemn manner. Michael takes a deep breath in apprehension then suddenly, the shimmering doors silently open, a piercing white light floods the halls of the palace, and the seraph Nathanael steps forward from the room. His six wings glisten in the warmth of the light, and his illuminated robe shimmers like a prism of color. Greeting the two archangels, he walks with them down the hallway.

"The council has come to a decision," he says, "The threat of the adversary is too great to ignore. The outright boldness of the demonic attack on the mortal plane has given us reason to believe that further confrontations may occur. We cannot allow these things to continue. Mortals who have given faith to our Lord, whose lives have been wrongfully taken by unholy creatures, are subsequently prohibited from entering our kingdom, regardless of any efforts of our kind to save them."

"So what must we do to prevent any further sacrilege?" asks Uriel.

"The council will call for every soul, who is willing to sacrifice their very divinity in the name of God, to prepare for the invasion of Hell itself. Every ounce of sin within that land shall be erased, unfortunate as it may be…"

"Why, Nathanael? Why is it unfortunate?" asks Michael.

"The balance of positive and negative energies will so greatly shift, most of the mortal world will be destroyed. Our angels, that reside among the humans, will see to it that some may survive so that they may procreate and rebuild their civilization."

Michael's eyes fill with dread as he glances away from the Seraph, and silently the trio continues to walk down the glistening hallway.

Nathaniel turns to Michael once again and adds, "We have already sent a party into the dark to deliver our message to the Great Betrayer. I highly doubt he will surrender quietly.

***

In the black palace, Crissella and Jezebel uncomfortably pace around the room. They both show signs of worry on their faces.

"She is more steadfast than her appearance leads one to believe, I am almost certain she was able to defeat them... much like the Minotaurs." Jezebel says.

"She would have returned by this time. Her wisdom would tell her to get away from that place as soon as she could," Crissella dictates as she looks into her mirror; suddenly her face distorts with rage and then she smashes her fist into her reflection, shattering the glass.

"I can not believe they tried again to murder us! That bitch will suffer my wrath, or so help me I will bring this palace down trying!" Crissella yells.

Jezebel stops pacing and says; "This palace may come down sooner than you hope for, sister. That attack could not have been viewed with tolerance by angelic eyes." Just then the sisters hear a great commotion erupting from outside the palace. They look at each other nervously before they run into the hallway to find the source of the shouting. Once they reach the nearest window, the sisters look down to see a large gathering of demons and unholy creatures that spout the foulest of obscenities and insults at a small company of angels who walk toward the palace doors, protected only by a halo of light. The two archangels Gabriel and Raziel escort the seraph Kemuel while two lesser angels follow behind them.

The company closes in upon the doors and demand to be let in.

"I command that you open your doors so that we may enter," Raziel shouts. Immediately the doors to the palace creek and grind open, rust and dirt, cake and fall from the gnarled bolts and spikes that decorate it. The company walks patiently by the growling demon guards that line the hallway until they reach the dark prince's courtyard.

Crissella and Jezebel perch themselves on a ledge overlooking the throne room as they eagerly examine the intrusion. The throne is empty and only a few guards stand around the outer walls of the room, and the archangel Gabriel calls out, "Stand before us, Betrayer! Your presence is demanded!"

The thundering voice of the dark prince replies to the archangel's command:

"For what reason do you befoul the borders of my kingdom?"

The seraph Kemuel answers, "The seraphim council has judged your attack upon the mortal world as an attack against God himself, and thus actions are to be taken which will prevent any further confrontations."

"What... actions?"

"Your kingdom shall be invaded by the Lord's army so that your existence shall be purged from the universe and your influence stripped away!" replies the confident Seraph.

In a burst of scorching hellfire, Satan himself appears before the angels in his true, horrible form. With a roar of anger that shocks the palace, he thunders within inches of the company. The beast stands thirty feet tall by mortal standards, and his shadow blankets the room in the grim darkness.

"You dare to enter my kingdom declaring an act of war? Let your forces come, for I will lay waste to every last soul who challenges me! My minions are the fiercest creatures in the universe; your weak, groveling sheep will stand no chance against the fury of Hell!"

"You had best prepare yourself quickly, for at the shift of the solar tides... the purification will commence." Kemuel explains. Satan releases a roar of fury before the angels that shake the mountains surrounding the palace, and then Kemuel commands:

"Gabriel, Raziel we must return to the shining city. Let us depart from this forsaken land." The Company of angelic messengers turns and marches down the hallway from which they entered. In his frozen throne room, Satan says to his general:

* * *

"Raise the troops. Tell them to prepare for Armageddon!"

The sisters, Crissella and Jezebel look at each other in apprehension; they quickly leave the throne room and return to their chamber.

***

Meanwhile, on the mortal plane, freezing sleet sears the nighttime air, as Celestial lies inside of a ventilation shaft on top of a small building. With her wings wrapped around her body, Celestial sleeps patiently, in wait for Michael's return.

Suddenly, the darkness of the ventilation shaft is illuminated by a soft glow of warm light. Celestial looks towards the source of the illumination only to see Michael's radiant face gazing back at her.

"I said I would return. Never will I surrender my love for you, Celestial."

"I dreamt of you in your absence. The love that burns in my heart, has kept me warm through the night." Celestial says as she calmly crawls out from the ventilation shaft. Michael places his arms underneath her cold body and carries her tenderly to the corner of the rooftop where he sits with her. Michael radiates a Heavenly energy field from his mind's eye and deflects the stinging sleet away from them. As the lovers hold hands Celestial presses her head against Michael's chest, she asks him:

"So, what happens now?"

Michael hesitates for a moment before disclosing the answer to her, "The Final Judgment. My brethren are preparing the army that will invade the forsaken land. At the shift of the solar winds… we attack."

Celestial sighs in anguish before saying, "Whom will they target?"

"Everyone." utters Michael, "Worse yet, the shifting of power in the universe will raze this world to the ground, along with Hell itself. The seraphim council have justified the sacrifice by appointing the earthen angels, who reside among the mortals, to see that they survive and repopulate the planet."

"It is true then, another level of the angelic hierarchy does exist. May God have mercy on all souls," Celestial mumbles as a tear of sorrow falls from her cheek.

"If only that were possible," Michael says as he holds his head against Celestials. The couple rests together in silent dismay, when

Michael says to her, "Celestial, you must know that there is a very real possibility that we may never see one another after this night."

"Oh, Michael.   No matter what happens, our memory will echo throughout the universe for all time.   If we must die now, then let us make our last night together, special!" utters Celestial as she leans in to tenderly kiss her lover upon the lips.   Michael strokes her hair as she grasps his body; the couple gently presses their foreheads together and unites their souls through the mind's eye.   As if in a trance, the lovers sit motionless with their eyes closed while the passion of their love flows throughout their bodies.

***

In the black palace, the sisters Crissella and Jezebel lay in an embrace of unconditional love while they weep in sorrow, knowing that their world is soon coming to an end.

"Do not fear our fate, Jezebel, I will stay by your side until the very end," Crissella says to her weeping sister.

***

Just beyond the steps of the palace, the dark army of Hell rises from the soil.   Countless thousands of beasts and horned demons emerge from the acrid ground and the smoldering pits.   They forge their armor and weapons from hellfire as they yell and roar to rally their fellow minions.   There are massive lumbering beasts, made of molten rock, that step forth from the Lava Rivers, searing paths through the ground. Demonic riders, who harness unholy dragons and blazing horses with six legs, blacken the skies like a plague of locusts.

Satan, himself, steps out from his palace in the armor of a black knight, in which only his flaming red eyes are visible through his spiked helmet.   His equally fearsome general, Morbidus stands beside him.

"Today is a good day for death, General!   Those impotent sheep will soon understand what it means to be hell bound!"

"Yes, Master.   With little effort, we will vanquish those pathetic creatures!   Our numbers climb greater than ten times one-hundred thousand and we continue to grow every hour."   Morbidus says while they scan with pride the blackened fields of creatures and warriors, whose yells resound throughout the kingdom.

* * *

***

In the shining city, the archangels and dominions rally their fellow warriors, in preparation for the final battle. Mortal souls who choose to fight in the name of God, gather their holy armor and their weapons while they pray for protection. Angelic riders harness creatures of light, such as unicorns and white griffins, and fill the sky with their countless numbers. The city is abuzz with activity as souls from all around celebrate the coming fall of Hell, while others pray for their comrades in arms.

On the mortal plane, Michael and Celestial achieve the climax of their union, causing their souls to erupt with spiritual pleasure. The two wake from their state of trance breathing heavily from the rush of energy that flowed through their soft bodies, as they lovingly gaze into each other's eyes. Holding Celestial's hand, Michael stands up to say:

"With all my heart, Celestial, I love you. I will fight courageously so that peace may return to this world, as it was before the Creation."

"I will pray for you, Michael… and myself as well. I must find my sisters and lead them out of there before it is too late." Celestial says with determination. A sudden bolt of lightning splits the air and the crack of thunder that follows causes the lights in the city to flicker. A storm is coming.

"The balance of power is already shifting. I must return to Heaven. If I must die, I will die thinking of you." Michael and Celestial passionately kiss once again before he leaps off of the rooftop and soars through a portal to Heaven, to face battle. Celestial stands on the rooftop, watching him vanish from the Earth, while the sleet falls, and the lightning flashes.

CHAPTER EIGHT

The Final Judgement

In the dimly lit bedchamber, Crissella and Jezebel have no tears left to sob. They now stand in defiant determination as they plan for the coming devastation.

"If our lives must come to an end today… that unholy wench, Eva will end with us!" Crissella growls, with a sneer of hatred upon her face. Jezebel walks toward her and asks:

"What do you propose we do to her?"

"I have something special planned. Come, we must conjure the tool of her demise!" commands Crissella. The sisters leave the chamber and enter a pitch-black room at the end of the hallway.

Meanwhile, in Satan's forsaken bedroom, Eva herself gives her king further encouragement before he rides out to battle.

"Know this, you are the only creature in this land whom I truly love. My black heart will burn in pride for your victory over the angelic hordes!"

"It shall be my sword that will burn the hearts of angels this day! Some of the suffering bodies I will save so that you may feast upon their agony."

"I look forward to it, my love! Make them suffer a fate like none that could ever be imagined! It makes them that much more tender." Eva snarls.

"I will bring to them unimaginable pain, for they know not who they challenge!"

Satan walks with pride out of his bedroom to join his faithful troops on the battlefield. The hordes of demons and vile creatures are gathered around the palace, awaiting their master. From the main gate, Satan gallantly rides out upon his flaming, six-legged steed. Wielding his mighty sword that burns with hellfire, the dark knight addresses his army.

"Minions of Hell, prepare yourselves for a splendid battle! Today you shall face our most hated enemy, and today you shall bring him death. Tonight you will shed your blood so that the universe will forever remember this night as the night the shining city fell!"

His army erupts with earth-shaking cheers as they hold their weapons toward the sky and chant his forsaken name in their demonic tongue.

"Go forth my legions, and prepare yourselves for absolute victory!"

With an equally thunderous cheer, the army of demons thunder towards the open ground where they will confront their angelic enemies. The beasts and creatures chant and sing their satanic battle hymns as they march onward.

***

In Heaven, the divine warriors blare their silver trumpets as their marvelous army marches towards a safe location, far away from the shining city. Michael and Uriel stand atop a glistening mountain as they oversee the advance.

Uriel says to Michael, "It is truly a spectacle to behold; more than a million strong heading into the dark lands! Our lord's army marches forward to face the enemy, and on his ground, they shall defeat him. Those wicked creatures have not a breath of hope."

Michael is not quite as confident though, as he watches the flowing river of souls beneath him, "I feel uneasy about this, Uriel. Something seems wrong with this course of action… something unforeseen."

"You must have faith, brother… the seraphim council has ordained this action with our Lord's permission. With his infinite wisdom and strength behind us, there is no risk of failure," Uriel says, placing his hand upon Michael's shoulder.

"Your word I will accept, brother, though I am still troubled by this decision," Michael says.

"Your doubts are a virtue, it means that we are still better than the dark spawn beneath," Uriel responds as the troops arrive at their destination, "It is time, my brother."

The two archangels draw their illuminated swords and place their golden helmets on their heads. Uriel shouts out to the army before him:

"Heavenly soldiers, prepare yourselves to fight against most feared adversary our kind has ever known! Together we shall purge this universe of his evil henceforth! Be not afraid of oblivion for God's love and wisdom follows you into the darkest corners of the universe."

The army cheers in excitement when Raziel flies before them. The archangel holds his sword high in the air and yells, "The gateway to the forsaken land shall be opened! Go forth and face your destiny for the sake of all that is good!"

The white clouds before the army suddenly crackle and twirl as the inter-dimensional portal open to Hell. Before the army charges forward, Michael makes one last request to Uriel.

"When we engage in battle, I ask only that Lucifer fall by my sword! My vendetta against his traitorous soul is personal!"

"Whatever you wish, my brother," replies Uriel.

***

In Hell, there is a disconcerted lull over the soldiers as they stand and wait for the invasion to begin. Some creatures inspect their weapons and their armor, while others stand patiently and determined. Suddenly, a crack of lightning scorches through the sky as the ashen clouds swirl into a vortex above them. A white beam of light penetrates the sky, instantly bringing Hell's army to a deafening roar. The beasts clash and rattle their weapons in defiance, as the clouds open.

Satan's attention is drawn towards the light when he says:

"At last, the end has come!"

From Heaven above, a collective battle cry echoes throughout the land as the army of divine warriors rain down from the sky. Arrows, burning bright with blue fire, whistle towards the demonic army below. Like a swarm of insects, the winged beasts take flight and confront their enemies. The opposing forces collide in a shower of lightning. Hundreds of bodies, both divine and evil, fall from the sky, lifeless, and smash into the dry soil below.

The angels that reach the ground are quickly cut down by the hordes of demons, which swing their deadly, flaming weapons in unadulterated fury. Both clear and black blood gushes forth from the bodies of the slain, soaking the ground with death. Demons tear the wings from angel warriors, transforming them into demons themselves. The masses of beasts, at ground level, quickly become overwhelmed by angelic warriors who stab and slice a path through the sea of enemies.

From above, Michael bursts through the portal to witness firsthand the horrendous carnage, taking place. The flood of angels into the forsaken land can be compared to a raging waterfall, crashing down upon jagged rocks.

Uriel joins Michael as they hover in the sky, "Lord have mercy! Their numbers are far greater than we had anticipated."

"That is all the more reason why we should fight with all of our strength. Look, the demons are transforming our soldiers into their minions. They are turning against us!" Michael shouts.

Uriel stares in disbelief when he finally says, "How is this possible? Each warrior they take becomes one more that we must fight!"

"We must not allow ourselves to be turned, Uriel. We must fight as we have never fought before my brother!" Michael shouts before charging through the cloud of winged creatures, slicing and stabbing those that get in his way. He soars further across the battlefield until he spies the target of his vengeance. Satan rears his steed up on two legs and lets out a deafening battle cry.

Michael perches himself upon a mountain top where he yells, "Lucifer! Come forth and face your end!"

"You dare utter that name, Archangel!   I will tear you limb from limb before I feast upon your bones!"

Satan and his steed take flight in an orb of fire. Michael charges the dark knight with his sword over his shoulder in preparation for the swing. The two enemies clash their blades together with unyielding fury, spitting blasts of raw energy from the parry, as they violently try to destroy one another. Satan's blade trails with hellfire as he swings at the elusive Michael. The battle rages on.

***

Farther away from the mass chaos, Eva stands in front of her window, overlooking the devastation. From behind, the sisters Crissella and Jezebel barge into her room. Eva turns and faces them in surprise

"How dare you maggots violate my privacy? You are supposed to be out there, dying for your master!"

Crissella steps forward, with fire in her eyes, as she says; "I would never put my life in danger for that bastard husband of yours!"

Jezebel steps forward to join Crissella when she says to Eva, "Beside the point, the only creature destined to die in this room, is you!"

"You dare threaten my life? I can destroy you pathetic creatures with my bare hands!" Eva shouts.

Crissella stares the queen in the eyes and responds, "Perhaps, which is all the more reason why we have resurrected a little friend of yours!" At that moment one of the Minotaur guardians that once stood outside of Eva's chamber, bursts through her door, shattering the frame into hundreds of pieces. The creature smashes his ax into the walls and through dressers as he roars in anger.

"You should remember this creature, Eva, except this time he is loyal only to us!" Crissella steps aside to let the beast step forward.

The Minotaur roars at Eva as he raises the ax above his head. Eva quickly dives out of the way, as the demon smashes the weapon into the floor. He swings several more times, but the evil queen ducks and rolls, narrowly avoiding the strikes. Eva soon finds herself trapped in the corner, looking up at the towering beast.

Without hesitation, the Minotaur lifts his ax one last time as Eva screams in terror. The massive beast brings the ax down with tremendous force, instantly crushing Eva's body, splattering her black blood across the walls of the bedchamber.

The Minotaur releases his blood-soaked ax and faces his mistress, Crissella. He obediently crouches down upon one knee to await her instructions.

Crissella steps forward and addresses the humble beast, "Congratulations, you have completed your task, my faithful servant. I now set you free!"

With a kiss upon the creature's forehead, he releases a dying moan as the fire in his eyes burn away. The creature's body falls into itself and becomes no more than dust that blows away.

***

Meanwhile, on the mortal plane, Celestial tries to safely navigate the devastation that is taking place around her. The start of the war in Hell has shifted the power balance so greatly that the Earth itself is being destroyed by mass, natural and unnatural disasters. Buildings topple like cards, while violent lightning storms ignite buried fuel reserves around the cities. People scream in terror as they run for their lives throughout the streets.

Celestial takes flight from the rooftop as the building underneath her falls into itself. As she ascends higher into the air, Celestial can see disaster for miles across the Earth. The horizon glows with a sickening green color as the energy from Hell bursts through the ground.

"God, why must this be the fate of the world?" She asks before she flies toward a safer location. Bolts of lightning strike around her while she weaves in between various telephone poles and buildings that subsequently plummet to the ground; explosions light up the nighttime sky from the many gas stations in the city. With much relief, Celestial identifies a subway entrance that she can dive into, to hopefully shield her from the destruction.

Deep inside the subway, people continue to run in panic as the trains de-rail from their tracks and hurtle into support columns, making the roof very unstable. Cement, metal, and glass decimate the interior of the facility as Celestial quickly lunges into a bathroom where she can buy enough time to conjure a portal back to her world. Celestial orates the satanic spell that opens the flaming gate to Hell, though she has little time to acknowledge the devastating war taking place on the other side, and so she falls forward into her homeworld. The subway ceiling collapses, mere seconds after Celestial enters the portal.

In a burst of flame, Celestial breaks through to the plane of Hell where she is rendered silent by the scale of devastation that spans across the land. A deafening bombardment of screams and clashing steel echoes throughout the air as Celestial questions where to fly. The sheer brutality of angels slaying demons and demons slaying angels is almost unbearable while Celestial flies from the fields of death towards the unholy palace. The sky quakes of fire and lightning with a supernatural resonance, as Celestial, hurtles through the black canyons. Boulders and shattered debris fall from their peaks, while Celestial weaves from side to side.

Mere yards away from the end of the canyon, a tremendous bolt of lightning strikes the mountain face with surgical precision, causing it to violently explode in a blast of stone and smoke. Celestial flies as quickly as she can to escape the ensuing rockslide, but is quickly overtaken by the debris. Large chunks of rock smack into her body, causing her to fall to the canyon floor, where her violent impact renders her unconscious. Falling rocks bury her alive, shutting out all light from the battle beyond, and with it, all hope.

CHAPTER NINE

The Revelation

Armageddon has, at last, come to the forsaken land, and Hell soaks with the blood of the slain warriors. The souls that have been damned to Hell, for their sinful lives on Earth, break free of their bondage and take flight from their captors, for the beasts that once guarded them have since been pulled into the bloody conflict upon the fiery plains. The bodies of fallen warriors continue to litter the ground, while a never-ending surge of angelic warriors rains down from Heaven.

Michael and his nemesis, Lucifer the Fallen, daringly battle one another with unyielding resolve. The skies above them burst and crackle with violent bolts of raw energy when, suddenly, another portal opens through the clouds. Satan knocks Michael away long enough to witness the event.

"Do you see? The lost souls from Earth fall into my kingdom by the millions. Watch now, as they become my unquestioning soldiers!"

With a burst of energy Satan engulfs the new souls in hellfire, instantly transforming them into winged warriors of Hell. As they fall, the new creatures quickly spread their wings and join the battle in progress. Weapons formed from Hellfire, materialize in their hands as they crash into the stream of angels, thus adding more bloodshed to the mayhem.

***

In the palace, away from the battle, Crissella and Jezebel run through the halls as the structure around them crumbles. Statues fall from their pedestals, shattering upon the floor, while the moats of blood within the throne room overflow across the floor.

"We must flee from here, sister... the divine ones will be here shortly!" Crissella yells to Jezebel.

"Let us take the underground passage that leads toward the mountains, we will be safe there," responds Jezebel. The sisters turn down a small corridor that splits off from the main hall, but as they run towards the rusted gate at the end of the path, a large boulder crashes through the wall before them. The voices of archangels can be heard just outside, but the sisters lunge for the gate, regardless. Crissella slashes the lock from the chain and they enter the tunnel, leading toward freedom. The roof of the main throne room crashes to the ground behind them while the echoes of the suffering souls reverberate throughout the halls.

***

Meanwhile, in the shattered ravine to the south of the palace, Celestial lays unconscious under a pile of rock and soot, where her mind reels in a dream-like state. She finds herself enshrouded in darkness as she calls out for any soul that may be near:

"Hello, is anyone there? What is this place, where am I?" Celestial feels around in the darkness, looking for any possible exit when suddenly a piercing beam of white light shines down upon her. The demoness looks up with her hand over her face to block the overwhelming brightness and warmth that flows from it. A soft, genderless voice emanates from the light.

"Be not afraid my child, for I do not seek to bring harm unto you."

"Who speaks to me? What do you wish of me?" asks Celestial as she winces from the light.

"You speak to someone whom you have known since your creation, and yet this only is the first time you have truly spoken to me. I have always been watching you, though you have never seen me. I have always heard you, yet you have never heard me. Look within your heart and my identity shall be made known to you."

Celestial looks around in anxiety as she struggles to find the answer within herself, and then suddenly her eyes fill with tears when she realizes whom the voice belongs to.

"You are my Lord… God."

"I am, the one." the being replies. Celestial falls to her knees in angst as she stares at the light.

"Why have you come to me, and now of all times? I have been cast out of the sanctity of Heaven for my sins! I have spoken blasphemy against you, and yet you come to me now."   Celestial cries as she awaits an answer.

"You may have been exiled from my divine kingdom… but you have never been exiled from my heart."

"I do not understand! I committed a great sin and you cast me from your grace," Celestial replies as she stands up in apprehension.

"Have I? Uriel became overzelaous perhaps, but never have I cast you from my grace. Does the Sun cast the Earth from its light? While it may vanish beyond the horizon, does not the Moon reflect it's glow throughout the nighttime sky? You may not be in my presence, but that does not mean that my love is withheld from you, my child."

With an even more confused look upon her face, Celestial ponders God's metaphor when finally she replies, "Why then have there been so many souls condemned to this dark place? Why then do they fall from grace for their sins?"

"Hell is a fate that only you can accept for yourself. Those who burn here have brought their suffering upon themselves by surrendering unto their guilt and fear. There are many misguided souls who wish to plant false accusations into the minds of the innocent, so that they may conform to a certain belief, but my love is reserved even for people such as those. Those of another faith exist on another plane, one which represents their belief and even on those planes, my love is reserved for them."

"You mean to say… I caused myself to fall from divinity? I spent countless hours praying for your forgiveness, but my prayers were never answered," says Celestial.

* * *

"Your prayers were never answered because your guilt would not let them be answered. Your prayers for forgiveness were in vain, regardless, simply because forgiveness had already been given to you."

Celestial falls to her knees, in tearful joy, as those words flow from God's heart. She sits there, quietly sobbing when the One says to her:

"Child, you must come to realize that I have no need to forgive fallen souls because judgment has never been cast upon them. The only heart to ask forgiveness from... is your own. Even angels, in all their divinity, are susceptible to emotions, such as anger, lust, or jealousy. These things are natural to you, for that is how I created you. Ask yourself why I would judge a soul for feeling those things with which I have blessed them?"

"I understand now, my Lord, but the war has already begun... what can possibly be done to stop this mindless suffering?" Celestial asks.

"You must bless their ears with this knowledge, that I have bestowed upon you. You must have faith in yourself, and not in me, to end this conflict. Go now my child, awaken and be free!"

With a burst of light the darkness that surrounds Celestial explodes with light at the moment she regains consciousness. Her eyes open and burn with blue a blue flame, as she effortlessly erupts from the pile of rocks that encase her. With newfound strength, Celestial launches herself into the air, easily clearing the heights of the black mountains; her demonic body glows with a white aura as she glares at the intense battle before her.

"I must have faith." utters Celestial as she hurtles herself forward toward the very heart of the chaos. Blazing by winged demons and fellow angels, Celestial streaks the sky with a white contrail behind her. Angels who try to strike her down are met with a blast of energy that knocks them from the sky; Celestial screams through the air at incredible speed as she flies toward the center of the battle.

The soldiers, charging from both sides, continue to slaughter each other while Celestial finds a plateau among the chaos where she can safely land. Celestial swoops down and lands with great force upon the surface where she then flails her arms in an attempt to draw attention from the fighting souls.

"You must cease, immediately! There is no need for this war to continue, I have just spoken to the Lord Almighty and…" she stops when she realizes that no one is paying her attention, a moment of hesitation slips by when she suddenly crouches down on one knee.

"My Lord give me strength," Celestial prays as she jumps to her feet, drawing every ounce of energy from the very Universe itself. Her halo of light burns brighter than any star in the sky as Celestial looks toward the Heavens and conjures a blast of light that pierces the fabric of the astral plane. The soldiers clench their ears in agonizing pain as the very foundation of Hell quakes from the roar of the power she has unleashed.

Satan and Michael hastily cease their fighting when they too clench their ears in pain. Jezebel and Crissella, who have just reached the surface of Hell from their underground tunnel, fall to their knees.

The blast of power sears the sky with a blue halo that crackles through the black clouds. Celestial looks toward the soldiers below her. They pay her attention now as the massive armies gaze at Celestial, standing upon the plateau.

The freshly invigorated demoness walks forward towards the ledge and orates to the crowd:

"This paltry war must cease! There is no rationale for this quarrel to take place upon a battlefield. I have just spoken directly to God himself and he has beseeched me to end this battle!"

"What blasphemy do you speak of, demon? You would never be allowed to speak to our Lord!" shouts a random angel from the crowd below.

"Who are you to dictate the words of God to us?" yells a demon from across the field. The agitated crowd murmurs and shouts at the statement made by Celestial.

"You must understand brothers and sisters, the conflict between good and evil should be fought within your heart! It should be fought with love and compassion, not blades and maces! Whether you're a demon or an angel, there will always be a speck of good or evil within your souls, for this is the way that God created us!"

Across the field, Michael recognizes who the distant speaker is, "Celestial, what are you doing?" Michael flies closer to hear her voice and the words she speaks, while Satan hovers in discontent. The mortal sinners, who have escaped their chains of bondage, flock to the radiant creature upon the plateau, like sheep that flock to the water.

They appear not as murderers or criminals, but as feeble victims, who have suffered years of brutal torture and labor.

Celestial continues orating to the endless field of creatures and angels, "For those of you who have begged forgiveness from God, beg no more for you have already been forgiven. You must only seek forgiveness from your own heart, and only then will you be set free from damnation."

The angels and demons look around in astonishment as some of the creatures begin to drop their weapons and unlatch their armor. One of the pitiful souls from below shouts out:

"What about Satan? He will not allow us to leave for he will surely destroy us!"

"Be not afraid of his wrath, for his power only exists through your fear! The Prince of Lies is a fitting title for that creature, for his threats are just that! You only have the power to free yourself from this land… do not surrender to your feelings of guilt and self-loathing, for you are all precious in the eyes of God. Look deep inside your heart and see the truth in the words that I impart to you this day. Go now and join your lord in Heaven who awaits you all with open arms!"

With those words, tremendous light bursts through the blackened sky as the crowd of demons and angels reel back from the luster. The beam shines down upon a small open space on the ground, and the creatures and angels stand around in amazement as they shout and murmur to each other. Some of the demons are frightened because they fear another attack from the shining city, but a single ragged and beaten soul who looks to have suffered countless millennia, timidly steps toward the light. He looks up and then holds his hand in the soft glowing pool of energy.

"It's so warm, yet it doesn't burn!" The man says as he cautiously steps into the light. In an instant, the withered soul is gently lifted from the ground as he rises towards the shining city. The man shouts and cries in joy as he ascends further into the light. The demons that stand around the beam are dumfounded while they witness the miracle before them.

Suddenly, more souls begin to step into the light, and they too are lifted into salvation. A winged demon, which has been cut and beaten during the battle, sheds his bloodstained armor and steps forward into the light, instantly transforming from his demonic self into a fair-skinned man as he too floats to Heaven above.

Celestial smiles while a tear of joy rolls down her cheek, and masses of demons and condemned souls begin to walk into the beam of light. There are some creatures amongst the crowd, who have fallen from Heaven like Celestial, and there are some who have never laid eyes upon the golden palace of God, but now they are all being saved from their suffering. Michael hovers in stunned disbelief as he witnesses the miracle, while rivers of souls march towards the ever-expanding beam of light to join their comrades in the holy land. All of the angels, who have fought so violently, drop their weapons and tenderly escort the weakened souls of both mortal sinners and enemy demons to Heaven with them.   Others carry the bodies of the slain towards the light where they are resurrected from oblivion to see their home once again.

Satan snorts and huffs in anger as he looks at all of his slaves walking into the light.

"Cease your treachery this instant! You will not walk away from me. I will not hesitate to destroy you all!"

Not one creature stops to acknowledge Satan's empty threat, so he sets his eyes upon a new target. Satan glares at Celestial who still stands upon the plateau.

"Bitch, if my slaves can't suffer for the rest of their existence... I will take as much pleasure by ending yours!"

The evil king roars in fury as he bursts from his black armor, exposing his true form. The beast increases his size three-fold and from his back, fountains of liquid Hellfire spews forth, taking the shape of a pair of dragon-like wings, which span more than one hundred yards in length from tip to tip. Satan raises his sword in defiance as he envelopes his body in blazing hellfire; with a final roar, he lunges forward to destroy the puny demoness.   Michael sees his enemy attack and quickly pursues, although the massive demon is flying at a speed too great for Michael to keep up.

Celestial glances at Satan from the corner of her eye and turns to face him. Standing patiently, Celestial utters to the creature:

"I fear you no more!"   Moments before the unholy beast reaches Celestial to swing his sword, an equally powerful burst of blue fire engulfs her body, crackling and buzzing with energy, as her red eyes burn blue once again, and her tan skin becomes fair like snow; her leathery wings dissolve into the white-feathered wings of an angel.

Her tattered rags become a shimmering robe of white silk as she stands defiantly before the beast.

Satan ferociously brings his flaming sword down upon Celestial, only to strike a powerful energy barrier that shatters his weapon into countless pieces. The beast is knocked back across the field from the blast of opposing energies and the force of his weight gouges a mile long trench through the burning clay.

Michael finally reaches the plateau and stares in amazement at the transformation that has taken place to his lover.

"Sweet, merciful God, you have been redeemed! I never would have thought…" Celestial walks closer to Michael when she puts her finger against his lips.

"Shhh…" Celestial says as she tenderly kisses him. The angelic lovers embrace each other on top of the small hill as their united auras brightly glow around them. Suddenly from below, Crissella and Jezebel climb upon the plateau from behind, their eyes widen in amazement at the magnificent sight of their sister, when Crissella says:

"Celestial… you're alive. I thought we had lost you." Celestial looks over at her sisters with a beaming smile and says:

"It was the faith in your heart that brought you to me. You never would have lost me, sister." The two demonesses run over to their angelic sibling and lovingly wrap their arms around her. Michael steps away to let them have a moment by themselves, as he watches the crowd of angels and souls ascending into the portal of light.

Michael looks across the battle-scarred land to see the soulless demons made from rock, lava, and ash fall and crumble to dust as the hellfire burns out from within.

Crissella asks Celestial, "I suppose this means you shall return to your true home?" Jezebel stares at Celestial with watery eyes as she awaits the answer.

"Yes, my sisters… but when I do, you shall be by my side. Look out there and you will see that both demons and angels are free to enter the shining city."

Crissella and Jezebel gaze in wonder as they watch their demonic comrades enter the light and transform into divine spirits. Crissella turns back and says, "You mean we can finally see the shining city?"

"Yes, my sister… Salvation awaits you both. No longer will you be slaves to your desires. You shall be free to exist in peace. Come, we must meet our Lord!"

The defeated Satan slowly stands from his freshly gouged trench and limps away, looking back at the sisters in despair, as he traverses the lonely path back to his shattered palace.

Celestial, Michael and the two sisters all fly towards the light that shines from above. As they enter into the passageway, Crissella and Jezebel joyously cry together as they are whisked away towards the land of Heaven, and a sight, which they never imagined they would ever see.

CHAPTER TEN

Redemption

Safe at last in the warm glow of the Heavenly kingdom, the gathered masses of angels, souls, and former demons stand just outside of the golden palace in excited anticipation to see their Lord. The air is abuzz with enthusiasm and joy as the souls reminisce with one another about their previous lives spent in Hell, and how relieved they are to be free of Satan's grasp. Michael and Celestial stand at the bottom step, along with the other archangels, Uriel and Raziel. Crissella and Jezebel stand next to their divine sister, their demonic forms having been transformed into fair and beautiful citizens of Heaven.

The crowd murmurs for several moments when suddenly, the palace doors open and intense light billows from within. The crowd goes silent as they await the presence of their God. Celestial gazes into the light to see the shadow of a figure walking forth from the palace interior. The form is tall and slender with a lucent body that shimmers with all the colors in a prism. The genderless figure approaches the crowd, a train of cloud and light flow behind it. The being's eyes glow blue more intensely than the brightest nighttime star, and thus it speaks to the masses.

"Very welcome are all of my children to the shining city. I am greatly pleased to see that through endless trials of pain and suffering at the hands of the Dark Lord, you all have broken free from the chains of guilt and fear that restrained your hearts. Blessed are you all."

Celestial steps forward to bathe in the loving warmth that radiates from the holy being.

"For untold millennia have I waited for the moment when I could gaze upon your face with my own eyes. The love in my heart for you, burns brighter than ever before, for you have saved us all."

"Credit me not for your redemption, child. It was you who stood in the face of darkness and brought light to the void. It was your faith that gave you the strength to bring direction to the hearts of those who were lost. Step forward, Celestial and gaze upon my face."

Celestial walks upon the steps and comes to stand before God. She looks upon the being's face and reels back in shock. Celestial reaches out to touch the face of God when she asks, "How is this possible? Your face is mine!"

"It is possible, for you and I are one and the same. All my children and I are one and the same, for wherever you suffer, I suffer, and wherever you love, I too love. From my essence were you all created, therefore I am you and you are me."

The crowd murmurs in hushed astonishment as they hear the truth about their relationship with God.

"In the beginning of creation, formed from dust Adam and his partner Eve, who were tempted by the misguided archangel, Lucifer. Upon eating the fruit of the tree of wisdom, not only were their eyes opened to the truth, which I speak to you now, but also were they given love, compassion, fear, and guilt. Thus they fell to the ground in angst, and they died, but from their flesh, I formed an organism of a single cell and so began the chain of evolution of all things."

A sudden shroud of dread falls over Celestial when she says, "What is to become of the mortal world? The war in the dark lands brought about unimaginable devastation to the Earth!"

"Have faith in your heart, my daughter. The reforming of the Earth has already begun, and in three days, the Earth shall be as it was before this conflict. Those who were taken by unnatural means have been returned to their flesh and will awaken to the brightest sunrise, and the happiest day with no memory of the suffering that was brought upon their world."

"Ever since I fell from Heaven, I have been playing out my role in your divine plan." With a gentle nod, God concurs with her statement.

"Never was I truly in danger, I suppose?"

God shakes its head silently, while Celestial chuckles, "In all your infinite wisdom and with all that you have said, you won't even speak now?"

God simply shrugged.

With a sarcastic scoff, Celestial responds, "You are a comedian, after all!"

"What more did you expect of me, child? Humor is a gift that must never be lost from your heart."

The two beings chuckle together when Celestial goes to embrace the Holy Spirit, saying, "I love you!"

"Yes child, I know. Even when you said that your forgiveness would not be granted to me, never did I withhold my love."

When Celestial pulls her arms away, she notices a sparkling essence that seems to crawl up her arm. With apprehension, she looks into God's eyes for an answer.

"Be not afraid, for it is a gift! Through darkness and fire, you have proven your faith in yourself, and have brought these souls to redemption. For that, I extend my thanks."

The substance on her gown blows into a cloud of glittering dust that twirls around Celestial's body, lifting her into the air. Michael and the sisters, along with others, gaze upon the event before them. The dust glows brightly with a blue halo as it flashes and sparks with divine light. Her gown glistens with gold and jade while Celestial's angelic wings separate twice more into pairs, leaving her with six wings in total. From below, God announces to the gathering of souls:

"For her immeasurable good to this universe, I hereby bestow upon Celestial the authority of my Seraphim!"

Her aura now glows bright yellow, when Celestial floats softly down to the steps of the golden palace. Her dear friends run to her in amazement, bringing words of accolade.

Jezebel excitedly says to her, "My sister, you have become so beautiful! Your very face radiates with warmth."

Crissella steps up from below and says, "If ever there was an angel in Heaven who deserves such a gift, it shall be you! I cannot express how thankful I am for what you have done for us. You are a rose among thistles, you are an angel whom I will never be ashamed to call a friend." Crissella embraces her sister, while the crowd behind them cheer in celebration.

A male soul from the left shouts out, "For Celestial, our savior!" The massive crowd releases a grand cheer for Celestial, and celebrations soon follow. The souls of the redeemed dance and sing together in the streets of the shining city while angelic Cherubim play their golden harps and flutes.

Michael stands before Celestial with love in his eyes, "You have done such a respectable thing for our kingdom; there is no blessing that I can give you that is a great enough reward!"

"Michael…" says Celestial as she presses her hand against his soft cheek. The lovers embrace and kiss one another, and then Celestial turns to God once more.

"There is a question that burns in my mind, Lord. If I have been destined to bring peace to the universe, where then does your son, the Christ, play out his role?"

"He is here, and he is there, coming and going around the world, spreading my message of love to the peoples of Earth. There are many, who do not recognize him, and there are some who do not accept him, but he gives them his love, regardless. His role is of a different caliber, so to speak."

Celestial's eye is suddenly drawn to a shrouded figure standing in a window within the palace. The radiant man in white raises his hand in peace; a white light pierces through his palm, and he bows his head to Celestial, before vanishing from sight.

"My Lord, was it he whom I saw just now?" Celestial asks with enthusiasm.

"It was he. If you look with open eyes, you will see him around more often than you realize."

 Michael puts his hand upon Celestial's shoulder saying, "Today is a day for celebration, my love. You have brought to countless souls, something they have never felt before, freedom! Let us be merry with all of our brothers and sisters."

With a cheer from the immediate crowd that stands around the heroine, her smile of accomplishment quickly drains from her face when she turns to God yet again.

"What is wrong my love?" Michael inquires.

"Celestial?"

With a solemn tone, Celestial replies, "I have freed all of my sisters; I have freed all of my brothers, except for one."

***

In the desecrated kingdom of Hell, a vacant calm blankets the ashen land of sin. The rivers of lava have ceased flowing and have hardened into black rock. The weapons and armor, from redeemed souls, lay scattered across the black ground. The sky no longer burns with fire but quietly flows with acidic rain as the ground steams with toxic fumes. Satan's palace has crumbled to ruins, but within he sits on his broken throne in unendurable despair.   The rain lands upon his charred flesh as the defeated beast, sobs tears of dwindling Hellfire that burn the ground beneath him.

The darkened hallway before the dethroned king suddenly fills with light, and as he looks up to identify the source of the light, he is greeted with the silhouette of a six-winged angel. The light fades ever so slightly as Celestial herself emerges from the crumbling corridor.

Satan looks away in shame as he says to her:

"You have already left my kingdom in ruin. You have taken my souls from me. What more could you come to take?"

Celestial steps forward to meet the unholy creature as she replies, "I come to take you … Lucifer."

"I am no longer worthy of that name. It was that name which betrayed me, and cast me from God's presence!"

"That is not true… it is you who has cast yourself from the shining city. Never have you been judged for your sins, not even by God."

"I see how it is… you come here to mock me as part of some twisted angelic joke! You have taken everything from me but my dignity, and now you return for that as well."

"I do not come to mock you, Lucifer. I stand before you now to speak unto you the truth! Exiled from Heaven, though it may seem, never were you exiled from God's heart." Satan sits in bewilderment as he ponders Celestial's words.

"Tell me, angel, if our Lord has not exiled me from his heart… why then, did he wage war upon me?"

"He did not. The angels, who are as capable of making mistakes as any mortal, made the decision to wage war against you. God allowed this tragedy to happen only so all souls could realize the error of their ways."

From the shadowy hallway behind Celestial, a mangled and rotten body of a woman runs, screaming, toward the Seraph.

"Die, you angel bitch!" she yells as she attempts to strike Celestial with a rusted sword, but her strike only contacts the same energy barrier that Satan struck in the field. In surprise, he stands up to marvel at the sight of the mangled figure.

"Eva, you're alive?"

"Quit standing there like an imp and help me destroy this whore once and for all! Her traitorous sisters tried to kill me!" Eva yells as she continues to strike the energy barrier in vain, while Celestial calmly stands her ground.

Sparing him the briefest of glances she says, "See the hatred in her eyes. Is that what you wish to feel for the rest of your existence? I offer you a chance to redeem yourself with the one being who has never stopped loving you."

Satan looks back and forth between the two women as if trying to making a choice. Eva growls at him and says, "What is wrong with you? Why do you stand there, you pathetic little maggot? This angel trash has left my kingdom in ruins!"

Satan's eyes burn with fury as he hears Eva's remark, then he yells to her:

"Your kingdom? Ungrateful bitch, I raised this kingdom from the black rock beneath our feet! You were made from my very rib, therefore you too can be unmade!"

With a ferocious roar, Satan bursts with fury, illuminating his toppled throne room with the last remaining hellfire in his kingdom, as he takes up from the ground, a broken sword. With the last of his unholy energy, Satan makes the sword burst into flame as he angrily stomps over to Eva.

"What are you doing my love? Stay away from me, you would not hurt your queen would you?" Eva pleads as she backs into the corner of the room.

"I have tolerated enough of your arrogance, woman! I will now finish the objective that my slaves set out to achieve!"

With a single, fierce swing of his flaming sword, Satan slices his former queen right through the middle of her already mangled body. Her torso smacks against the wall while her legs fall to the ground before her; her black blood gushes from her dismembered halves. The cut has severed Satan's divine rib from her body, instantly causing her to dissolve and melt into a puddle of boiling black oil. Eva's unholy blood quickly crystallizes into a fine powder that blows away to nothing. Satan stands over his broken rib upon the floor, as he drops his shattered sword to his side.

Breathing heavily from the rush of adrenaline, he reaches down to grab the broken bone. Holding the rib in the palm of his hand, Satan stares in discontent while he says to the Seraph behind him:

"She was the first, and only, success that I could bring out of this cursed soil. I wanted nothing more than to have a partner who would love me throughout my darkest hours. Now I truly have nothing."

Satan falls to his knees, holding his head in angst. Celestial walks over to him and crouches down before him. Looking directly at the creature's hideous face she cups his cheek.

"There is something that you have, brother. Look into my eyes and see for yourself." The saddened beast slowly raises his head up to gaze into Celestial's radiant eyes. The blue fire that burns in her eyes, radiate so much love and compassion that not even Satan himself can be consumed by anger or hatred. The creature is so overpowered by Celestial's compassion; he bursts into tears.

"Tell me why I should be forgiven, after all, that I have done?"

"Do not seek a reason for forgiveness, Lucifer… in your Lord's heart, forgiveness has already been granted to you," replies Celestial as she wipes away a tear with her thumb. The tender warmth from Celestial's hand causes Satan to drop his head to the ground in overwhelming joy. Celestial allows the sorrowful creature to cry out his long pent up angst; finally, he is able to bring himself to her eyes again, and he says to her:

"Does he still love me?"

Bracing his shoulders, Celestial replies, "God has never ceased loving you." Celestial leans forward and kisses the beast on the forehead as her tear of compassion rolls down her cheek and falls onto his burned skin. Celestial stands back to witness the miracle that takes place before her.

The creature stares at his body, watching the charred and torn flesh heal itself. The burns and scars that once covered his body, vanish while Satan's face transforms to that of a fair young man, and the bestial horns fall from his cranium while his rusted armor glistens again in the glow of Celestial's aura. Two feathered wings painlessly emerge from his back, and once again, he has become a radiant archangel.

Celestial approaches him and says, "At last, your inner beauty reveals itself. Come, we must return home… Lucifer." A beam of light pierces the black clouds as a portal to Heaven swirls open in the sky. Lucifer looks up in joyous amazement when he replies:

"Yes, let us return home." The Seraph extends her hand and grasps Lucifer's when they swiftly take flight towards the portal. Flying higher than Lucifer has ever been within his own kingdom, he looks down to see the world itself implode into a great fissure that opens from beneath. The land that he once knew as Hell dissolves into a ball of ash and dust as the portal entrance closes behind them.

The angelic pair soars higher and faster through the white tunnel until they emerge into the kingdom of Heaven. Tears of joy gush from Lucifer's eyes, as he gazes upon the golden palace of his father for the first time in untold millennia.   God's voice echoes through the air saying to his once fallen angel:

"Welcome home… my son."

Afterward

Wow.
Just... wow.
I wrote... that.

I'll be perfectly honest, it's not quite as bad as I thought it would be after so many years... but what a cringe-fest. For the record, I was in a completely different headspace when I wrote this. I was Republican with a simple black and white view on morality and hadn't yet gone through my political and social crisis of faith. I don't want to think of myself as a misogynist, mostly because even in High School I got along with more girls than jock dudes and was always an empath, but some of the cultural misogyny I got from TV and comics I was into at the time definitely got internalized. I mean, I was reading Purgatory and Lady Death when I wrote this soooo...

But despite my shortcomings, some of my core beliefs still ring true through my writing even now. Themes of hope and redemption, sacrifice and forgiveness are just some of the things I find universally appealing to me. I've always struggled to get ahead and to become who I felt I was meant to be, even now, but fiction allows me to live out that fantasy in worlds of my own making. I am a product of Star Wars, Power Rangers and Sonic The Hedgehog Saturday morning cartoon, I love campy good vs evil stories but as I've grown I've found that moral complexity and grayness is more appealing to me simply because of how real it is.

I knew back in 2004 that the idea of 'forgiving Lucifer' would be controversial but I had yet to be exposed to anything remotely resembling social media as we know it today. I hadn't yet gone through my own personal descent into Hell and back to come out with a new perspective on the world that shaped my personal worldview, but reading it know I see so much more potential for a nuanced character, more akin to Tom Ellis' Lucifer in the hit TV series.

I mean, Satan was an absolute DICK in this story, again a byproduct of my limited perspective of moral grayness and hero/villain dynamics as they relate to each other. I can assure you, dear readers, that my revamped novel will have 110% more complex Lucifer in it and possibly even an 'enemies to lovers' plot for our dear girl, Celestial? If there's one thing I love about female gaze stories it's the dynamic ascribed to empowerment and understanding of complex emotions that are more than just face punching and mono-syllabic grunts. To those ladies or gender fluid writers out there who write these kinds of stories, thank you!

Also, Eva was criminally underutilized I felt. She deserves to be the baddest bitch in the Black Lands (because she's literally made from pure evil) but instead, I just sidelined her while the hubby goes off to fight? I mean, wow, damn dude. Yeah... sorry, 10/10 will definitely fix in the re-write.

Life is a journey, so I can't be too ashamed of my old stuff, because it was the first step into a larger world. I've gone through the meat grinder economically, politically, and spiritually and have read all manner of books from the Illuminatus trilogy by Anton Wilson, Robert Heinlein, David Icke lizard people to literal JFK research nonfiction books. I've got a lot of stories and ideas floating around inside my head to draw from, certainly more now than I had when I wrote this. I've seen things and had personal experiences that have played into some of my biases of course, but I've always been a 'let's see where this goes' kind of person and if it bears fruit, then good, if not I move on.

The bones of a story are here, it's basically what a first draft should be before a total rewrite, but like any true revision of a fictional work, I need to take what works for me and discard the rest, trim the fat if you will, so that I'm left with a tight plot and solid characters that are both nuanced and dynamic, not the two dimensional meat sacks that punch each other in the face for three chapters.

I can't say when my re-tooled masterpiece will be finished, but I can assure you that I'll be letting everyone know... loudly and with much gravitas. A writers gotta eat too, amirite? So stay tuned my fellow fantasy travelers and struggling writers, you haven't heard the last of me, or Celestial, and definitely not Lucifer. Oh no, the gang will be back with a vengeance and things will be 100% sexier, more ACTIONY, more SENSICAL PLOTTY! I know these aren't words, but you can trust me.

I'm a writer.

Preview: Shadowbringer

Disclaimer

What follows is an unfinished draft of the first chapter of my rewrite. This is not the final text.

It wasn't the fall itself that terrified her so much as it was the sudden absence of her Lord mother's light. Engulfed in flame and smoke, Celestial plummeted to the cracked mantle of damnation itself. The impact left her body all but shattered at he bottom of the crater. She'd never experienced agony before, but her screams announced the terrible new sensation to all of Hell.

She didn't recall when she'd passed out, but the crack of another bone repairing itself startled her awake. She was still at the bottom of the crater staring up at the burning, ash-filled sky. Her throat burned with dust and pain but she managed to speak just above a whisper.

"Why? How could you, brother? How could you do this to me?" She could still see Uriel's wrath shining in his eyes as he made the proclamation which damned her to Hell. It happened so fast, she couldn't even argue her innocence and now... she was gone, never to see her home again.

She gasped as another bone repaired itself sending a jolt of pain through her again. If this was to be her punishment then there was little choice but to endure every moment of it and so she did. Her wings were the last to heal, but her body was stiff and sore as she forced herself to sit up.

Once radiant white robes were tattered, burned and torn revealing solid flesh beneath. No longer was she a being of pure light, but meat and bone, almost human with all the sin and shame that came with it. The ground was solid and dusty between her fingers; there was a strange sort of permanence to it.

A muffled cry chilled her pulsing blood. She whirled to see what it might be, but there was only dirt and the walls of the crater around her. A long moment passed before the tightness in her chest began to loosen when another lower moan drew her attention to the other side of the crater. A crack formed in the dry clay, preceding a small cascade of dirt as a skeletal hand emerged.

She stood on wobbly legs, fear coursing through her as the rotting corpse clawed itself from its shallow grave.

"Save… meeee!" Its voice was shallow and full of pain as it crawled toward her.

"No, no stay away from me!" Her voice broke with panic but then another rotting hand grabbed her by the ankle. She screamed.

"Save us, Angel!   Why has God forsaken us?"   The corpse' jaw barely hung from its socket as Celestial thrashed and tore herself free from its weak grasp.

"Get away, get away!"

"It's dark, I'm scared of the dark. Why am I here?" Said another hollow voice.

In moments she found herself surrounded by damned souls crawling from the dirt of the crater she'd made upon her fall, each calling out to her, desperate for answers, for hope, none of which she could possibly give. Frantic in her escape, she spared no thought to the tortured souls as she scrambled toward the edge.

The squish of rotten meat and the crunch of brittle bones beneath her feet drove her need. Her wings were sore but she managed to flap hard enough to launch herself out of the crater. She collapsed onto her back on the dusty plains as the voices of the damned murmured after her.

"Don't leave us."

"Come back."

"Don't forsake us!"

She drew in a heavy breath as she forced herself to her feet again and put as much distance between her and that damned crater as possible. Unfortunately for her, the surface was no more hospitable. The winds blasted her with dust like tiny razors until she shielded herself with her wings.

There were many texts documenting Hell in the Heavenly library, but none of her research had prepared her for the absolutely horrific stench of it all. The air itself seemed intent on breaking her as the smell of rot and brimstone assaulted her nose. Sulfur and smoke drifted by in waves, all of which made her gag, which in itself was another unpleasant sensation she wouldn't wish on any soul.

She could see little through the dust clouds, but the terrain became rockier as she went and soon became small hills, then canyons, and mountains. Her feet carried her as far as she could go since she needed her wings just to see anything. Growls and howls echoed through the brutal air, no doubt from beasts and nightmarish horrors she didn't want to encounter, but she carried on.

***

As she made her way higher up the broken path, she heard small animals fighting and snarling, but as she approached they scampered away in a hurry. That made her glad she wasn't on the menu just yet, but it still gave her cause for concern. What really got to her were the disembodied voices drifting in from the winds.

"Fallen and alone… damned and forgotten… there is no hope."

"I can smell her fear."

"The shadows have spread… the end is nigh."

No matter where she looked, she couldn't see anyone around her, but the feeling of being watched made her skin pebble all the same. The rocky terrain crunched beneath her delicate slippers, which had been reduced to nothing but shredded silk and exposed padding from her trek. She wondered how long she'd been walking for. Did time even matter in this place? Angels were heavenly beings who couldn't die, as far as she knew, but even in Heaven they had cyclical celebrations. Why wouldn't Hell be any different?

Falling rocks forced her to stop and look up, dreading what she might see. Her heart raced but she couldn't see anything through the smog. A drop of something hot and wet splashed against her face, making her flinch.

When she wiped the droplet from her face, she gasped when she saw the red smear in her palm. Then another drop hit her, followed by another, and yet another until the sky opened up with a crimson red rain.

Blood.

Celestial gasped as the red began to stain and soak into her white robes, washing her in the sins of Hell for good. She threw her wings up to shield her from the worst of it, but it was a downpour and even then, droplets leaked through her brittle feathers.

She kept walking but the blood rain didn't subside; eventually she found a decent enough alcove in the mountainside that she could duck into and out of the horror. Hugging her knees to her chest, she watched the bloody droplets drip from the ends of her wings before joining the small river of blood rushing by her red feet.

It was awful, all of it! Despite her studies, every single part of Hell was just as bad, if not worse, than she'd imagined. The air was foul, undead nightmares crawled from the ground, beasts of indeterminate size and number roamed the land and the skies rained blood. Glancing down at her red stained flesh made the horror more real somehow.

She'd been cast out, damned, thrown away. There was nothing she could do and nowhere she could go that wouldn't end with her enduring some cruel torture at the hands of vile demons or even the other angels, the Fallen. It was tempting to hide under this outcropping for all eternity if it meant no one finding her, but as unrealistic as that thought was, an ear splitting screech cut through the air to remind her she wasn't safe anywhere.

Celestial threw herself down, the beast was frightfully close, but when she risked a glance at the sky she saw only the swish of black wings cutting through the bloody rain before disappearing again. A second roar came from farther away, which she hoped meant the thing was flying far away from her. She sat up again and shrank back against the wall, her chest tight with anxiety, but there was nowhere to go even if she wanted to.

She hadn't realized she'd dozed off until she felt the jab of something metal and sharp.

"Ow," she yelped. The first thing she noticed was the eerie quiet, it had stopped raining, but the tang of blood was still fresh in the air. The second thing she noticed was the red skinned horned demon glaring down at her with a short blade in her hands.

"Oh good, sister she's awake! Best luck for me; I love it when they struggle!"

Celestial gasped with terror as she threw herself back against the wall.

"Oh no, you're not going anywhere, girlie! Come here!" The black haired demoness lunged forward and grabbed her by the arms.

"No, stop! Get away!" She kicked and flailed but her captor was unnaturally strong, pulling her out of the alcove and throwing her to the ground as thought she were little more than a doll. Celestial slid across the blood slick path before turning over to the sight of the creatures sword at her throat.

"Go on, try to run. I love playing with my food," she said with a wicked smile. The black haired woman was muscular and almost human looking except for her clawed feet, leathery wings and backward bent knees. She wore crudely hammered armor that covered her most vital areas but didn't encumber her range of movement.

"Really, sister? Is that anyway to treat our guest?" The woman's voice was thick and sultry. Celestial turned just enough to see a second demon striding over to them.

Though similar in appearance, this demon looked human. Her skin was crimson like the others, but she wore her black wings around her shoulders like a cloak but her legs were straight and her feet narrow enough to wear armored boots like an Angel. She too had horns but they were small and barely visible tucked between the mess of raven hair that framed her round face.

"She's a Fallen, sister, and she's terrified," the woman said as she knelt down to look at her.

"That's what makes it fun! How often do we get to torment a Fallen? These patrols have been pointless but now I can actually enjoy myself!"

Celestial didn't make any move to flee but said, "I've done nothing to you, please leave me alone."

"Aww, girlie is frightened; look how she cowers," the demoness jabbed her sword at her, nicking her skin enough to draw a droplet of blood.

"Ow, please don't!" She pleaded.

The other woman sighed. "She cowers from you because you're being a bitch."

"Thank you!"

The woman sighed again before offering her hand. "It's alright, angel, we're here to help you."

Whatever she'd expected the woman to say, that wasn't it. She traded glances between them. "How can I trust you? This is Hell. You're both demons aren't you?"

"Yes, this is Hell," said the woman, "and technically only Jezelle is a demon, I'm a mortal who was uplifted to demon status but it's kind of a long story."

Jezelle groaned. "Do you have to give her our life story? Can't I just knock her out and tie her up?"

The other woman glared at her sister. "We're not knocking her out. Unless she tries to run," she looked down at her with a raised brow.

"I-I won't run… I promise," she managed to say.

"Well that's boring," Jezelle grumbled.

"What my sister means is that's 'good to hear'. Hell is dangerous enough for new arrivals, and we'd prefer not to endanger ourselves pursuing you."

Celestial didn't like the sound of that, but she couldn't quite argue the point either. She had no idea what else was out there in the wastes.

"Also if you think about running just remember that we're both stronger and faster than you and it wasn't too difficult to track you here from that massive crater you left out there."

"Oh, right. Wait, you mean you saw me trying to get away from those things coming out of the ground, but you didn't intervene?"

"Oh those undead morons can't hurt you. They're more annoying than anything, probably just bored and looking for a cheap scare. That's beside the point, we knew you'd be fine, you look like you can take care of yourself."

She found that oddly complimentary coming from a demonic not-quite-demon.

"We were more worried about the wyvernath finding you."

Her blood went cold. "The wyver… what?"

Jezelle came forward clawing at the air for emphasis, "Big ass dragons! Their wings blot out the sky and their screech can paralyze you with fear if you aren't prepared for it. Surely, you've heard them out here," she finished just above a whisper.

Celestial swallowed hard. "Yes, I've heard… something. I think I saw part of one through the smog, but that's why I've been hiding."

The other woman approached and put a comforting hand on her shoulder; despite her best efforts she flinched at the touch.

"It's going to be alright, I promise. What is your name, angel?"

"Cel… Celestial," she said hesitantly.

"A pretty name. I'm Chrisella and this is Jezelle."

"Uh… hi?" She gave a nervous wave to which Jezelle rolled her eyes with obvious annoyance.

"I know it's frightening. I was the same when I first came here, lost and scared like you, but I endured and found my way to where I am now. I can assure, you're better off with us than out there alone."

"And where would that be, exactly?"

Chrisella exchanged a glance with Jezelle. "We're with the

Luciferian Sisterhood."

Her breath caught in her chest. "Luciferian... you mean, you serve him, you serve Lucifer?"

"That's right. We're bodyguards, warriors, we put down fights or start them depending on the situation and we're available for whatever pleasures he might demand from us." Chrisella's smile curved wickedly upward.

She felt an uncomfortable warmth bloom in her cheeks at the way Chrissella said it and tried not to let her mind race with all the implications of those words.

"I'm an angel though, what will he do to me?"

"Whatever he wants sweet cheeks," said Jezelle, adding, "And you're gonna like it too."

"Jezelle please," Chrissella gave her an intense sideye..

"What? I'm just messin' with her, don't get your loincloth in a knot."

"We should get out of here, call them."

"On it," Jezelle said before blowing a sharp whistle near the edge of the outcropping.

Celestial turned to Chrissella. "Mounts? You rode here?" That seemed odd considering they both had wings but then she thought that hellions might get tired from exertion. There was a lot she didn't understand what became clear a moment later was the terror she felt as a massive gust of warm air announced the arrival of a massive winged serpent descending from the sky. Its long snout was all fangs and shredded meat as it let out a piercing shriek, the very sound she'd heard earlier.

Jezelle smirked at her. "These are our wyvernath. What did you think we rode on, unicorns?"

The great beast dug its claws into the crumbling rocks as its massive head veered toward her. Celestial wasn't able to form words even to scream; as she stumbled backward, the ground shook as a second great beast landed behind Chrisella. This one was considerably larger.

"It's alright Celestial, they won't hurt you. We were just having a little fun," Chrisella said.

"No, no, this is a trap. Get away from me; get away!" Reacting on pure instinct, she threw herself off the ledge and opened her wings to the searing wind in a desperate attempt to escape. The sisters curses followed her down.

"Shit!"

"Yes, now this is more like it, sister!"

"Shut up. After her!"

Her wings burned from the strain of keeping herself aloft. The physics of this world didn't agree with her and it took her a moment to level out but not before she rolled over long enough to see the black silhouettes of the wyvernath spreading their wings and diving after her.

She wanted to scream but her instincts kicked in and her resolve became clear. When she managed to control her fall, she soared away as fast as her wings could carry her, diving toward the canyon below.

"You're wasting your time, girlie but feel free to make it more fun for me!" Jezelle shouted as the shadow of her mount descended upon her.

Celestial looked over her shoulder to see the jagged teeth of the wyvernath glistening with rage. In a panic she closed her wings and tumbled down from the sky just short of being swallowed whole. When she opened her wings again she slowed but not before slamming into the leathery wing of a second wyvernath.

"Ahh," she cried out as her wing cracked upon impact. A moment later she was falling again until a clawed hand grabbed her by the wrist.

"Celestial, this is foolish! We're not going to hurt you," Chrissella called out to her.

"No, no! Get your claws off me, demon! I'm not going anywhere with you!" Celestial cried out as her wing wrenched hard to the left, but in that moment a feeling filled her, an instinct so strong and clear she acted upon it without question. A black spear manifested in her free hand which caught Chrisella by surprise.

"You're… an archangel?" The woman said with surprise.

She'd been so distracted Celestial struck and sliced the demons arm with the spear tip.

"Aghh!" Chrisella cried out as her grip faltered, then Celestial was falling again, only this time there was no one to catch her.

She watched the ground rush up to meet her and attempted to unfurl her wings but the shock pain that lanced through her made it impossible. For the second time today, Celestial impacted Hell's cracked and barren mantle as the comforting darkness of unconsciousness welcomed her back into its embrace.